I0604858

TEACH ME

TEACH ME

MASQUERADE CLUB
BOOK ONE

LILITH DARVILLE

Copyright © 2021 by Lilith Darville

This is a work of fiction. Names, characters, places, and incidents either are the product of the author's imagination or are used fictitiously, and any resemblance of fictional characters to actual persons living or dead, business establishments, events, or locales is entirely coincidental.

All rights reserved. No part of this book may be reproduced in any form or by any electronic or mechanical means, including information storage and retrieval systems, without written permission from the author, except for the use of brief quotations in critical articles or a book review.

eBook ISBN: 978-0-9917538-8-8
Paperback ISBN: 978-0-9917538-9-5
Hardcover ISBN: 978-1-998127-00-9
Audiobook ISBN: 978-1-998127-01-6

Cover Design by Atra Luna Design (www.atraluna.de)
Editing by Maggie Morris, The Indie Editor (www.indieeditor.ca)
Formatting by Kate Tilton's Author Services, LLC (www.katetilton.com)

DEDICATION

For my Neo

When the door opened, everything I wanted to say to Meredith, everything I'd rehearsed became two words.

"You're back."

A smile holding a hint of promise lit her face as if we'd parted three minutes ago, not three years.

I'd been eighteen when we first met. She was twenty-one. She took my virginity. She taught me to be a man. Then . . . three years apart. The inevitable realities of the world had little consideration for such passion.

Summer found me delivering prescriptions in the small town of Kincardine to earn my tuition. Staring at today's pink delivery slip was like stepping back in time—same name, same place. Meredith Kincaid, Sandvine Estate. Could she really be back? Would she be there when I rang the bell?

Get a grip, Connor. She might not even care to remember that summer. She might not—

My finger hovered on the doorbell. *Push it, you idiot.* I closed my eyes and rang. When she opened the door—in a bikini fit to tempt the gods—she answered my two awkward words with *five* words that changed everything, "I was waiting for you."

The moment I saw her, longing shot through me as if at last I'd found the cure for an itch I thought I'd forgotten. I stepped inside and stared at Meredith as she snatched the bag, tossed it on a nearby table, and closed the door.

"My God, you're beautiful." Desire licked at me like the touch of a match igniting a short fuse.

Her sapphire-blue eyes, luminous in the afternoon light, shone with anticipation.

Meredith pulled me into her arms. Her lips devoured mine as she ripped at my shirt in a fever of expectation. I smiled as I stepped from her embrace. I was no longer the awkward boy needing her to show me the way.

I took her hand and led her through the estate. Everything looked the same as it had three years ago. Her bedroom door stood open, and she yanked me into the room, tugging at my clothes. Even though my need was as urgent and savage as hers, I put my hands on her shoulders to still her.

"Slowly." I caressed the side of her face and tucked a tendril of hair behind her ear. Our time apart had changed me, and I wanted her to know it.

"I want you now, Connor." She clutched the back of my head and pulled it toward hers.

"Shhh." I held her at arm's length. "Not another word."

Meredith whimpered. Every fiber of her being trembled with impatience, and I smiled again. There was a time when the impatience had been mine.

I drew the angles of her face with my fingertips, delicately tracing the oval of her eyes, the rounded tip of her nose, and the lushness of her lips. When I stroked the backs of her delicate ears, she moaned. My skin heated at the sound. I inhaled deeply to still the fire threatening to consume me. Her dark hair cascaded down her back in waves. I took a handful, tipped her head, and brought her lips to mine.

I traced and retraced the outline of her lips with the tip of my tongue, eager to remember every contour of her exquisite mouth. Meredith's tongue joined mine, sending a jolt of lust through my aching hardness. She pressed into me, but I held her wrists at her sides.

Her impatience displayed her longing. I pulled her hands behind her back and held them with one hand before sliding my lips along the length of her neck. A wisp of her perfume made me stiffen, but I kept the reins on my control. Using my free hand, I untied the top string of her bikini. I gazed into her sparkling eyes, measuring her response while I inched the top loose and tossed it to the floor.

Meredith's breasts were magnificent, and I paused to admire them. My pulse quickened, but I managed to continue the measured pace of my breathing. I let go of her wrists and cupped the soft globes in my hands. Stifling a sigh, I studied the way the blush of her tan contrasted with the darker hue of her small, brown nipples. Meredith let out a low moan as my tongue circled each hard nipple before sucking them deeply, first one, and then the other. She arched her back, and her hands encircled my head. I licked and gently tugged each nipple until she stood on her toes, taut with longing.

Straightening, I looked into her eyes and was rewarded with tortured anticipation as I undid the sides of her bikini bottom. It dropped to the floor. As I picked her up, she wrapped her legs around my waist and buried her face in my hair. I carried her to the bed and took a moment to admire the perfection of her smooth, tanned skin against the brilliant-white duvet. Her need surrounded me, threatening to consume me. The look in her eyes begged me for release, but I wanted this moment to last for eternity. Her soft flesh warmed as I ran my hands over the curve of her abdomen and down the insides of her thighs. They came away wet with the essence of her desire.

She spread her legs wide for me, giving me the full view of her manicured pussy. I traced my finger across her clit. A small groan of satisfaction I couldn't suppress rumbled from the back of my throat. But when she reached for the button of my jeans, I pushed her hands away.

"This time I want to pleasure you."

I worked my jeans and briefs past slim hips, my gaze never leaving her face. Women appreciated my body, and I wanted her to see the man I'd become. Meredith licked her lips as my long, thick cock broke free of its prison. She reached for me. I shook my head ever so slightly. I'd dreamed of how this reunion would be, and I fully intended to make that dream a reality.

Her sultry lips were plump with her longing. I bent and brushed them with mine before turning my attention to her glistening folds. I sandwiched her crimson bud between two fingers and her legs parted further, inviting me to devour her. With a growl, in one smooth motion, I knelt between her legs. Bending, I pulled her rigid clit into my mouth, torn by my desire to taste her and the satisfaction of watching her come.

The need to have her pulsed through me. I thrust two fingers into the wetness flowing from her before licking her essence from them. *God, she tastes good.* Returning to her, I pressed my fingers on her swollen G-spot, pushing upward while also rubbing the bud deep between the engorged petals of her nether lips. Meredith's eyes closed. She arched on the bed, her long lashes fanned on her cheeks. And I felt the first spasm as my body screamed for release.

Focus, dammit, focus!

I took a deep breath and reached for the steel core of my

control. Meredith panted and writhed. I took my time so I could take her to the highest peak, the ultimate climax. I stroked, squeezed, and stroked some more until her body was rigid and dripping with sweat.

"Please," she begged. "Please, Connor."

I looked up, savoring the sexual power I exerted as she twisted in her eagerness. How I'd missed this woman and her ability to lose herself to her own desire, and that desire was for me. I was home after being lost in a world of obscurity.

Again, I dipped my head and took her pulsing clitoris into my mouth, torturing it to its full extension. I took my time; I had all the time in the world. Finally, I pressed my fingers hard against the roof of her vagina. Meredith lay suspended as if life itself were too much. Then, with a raw cry, she clenched around my fingers, and the power of her orgasm jolted through me.

I fought the animal urge to rut between her legs, letting my hot seed pump into her. I wanted to show her I wasn't the impetuous boy she'd known. Withdrawing my fingers from her slippery cunt, I brushed them across her lips, reveling in her eagerness to taste what she'd so openly given me. She sucked greedily, devouring every bit of her delicious come from my fingers. My penis almost burst with the agony of my erection, yet still I was patient.

Heavy with arousal, I retrieved the condom I kept in the pocket of my jeans. My cock answered Meredith's groan. I rolled the sheath over my bursting rod. Slowly, deliberately, I knelt again between her legs. She grasped my ass. My balls contracted. Pulling her arms above her head, pinioning her wrists with one hand, I used the other to grasp one of her breasts. With a single thrust, I dove into her.

She slowly folded into me, wrapping herself around me, a lock receiving the key designed for it. Her engorged core was everything I'd remembered and so much more. Here was another moment I wanted to preserve for all time.

I held myself rigid and resisted the beginnings of the orgasm deep within. I wasn't sure how much longer I could endure, but I was determined to enjoy every moment in her cunt as if it were my last. With purposeful restraint, I plunged inside her, deep and hard, slow and long, never once taking my eyes off her. I loved to watch her writhe with her greed for me.

I stroked, sometimes slowly, sometimes with mad abandon, each time, stopping myself before I reached the point of no return. Finally, she went rigid again, signaling the time to embrace our mutual release. As she howled with her climax, I clenched, drew in my breath, and lost myself as I erupted into oblivion.

Throwing my head back, I gasped for air while Meredith's warmth enhanced my pleasure. I'd waited so long to touch her, yet nothing had prepared me for the intensity of our reunion. She pulled me on top of her. I stilled, enjoying the crush of her breasts against my chest. We lay, heart to heart.

I clung to the moment as if the hope of having joy in my life depended on it. Rolling onto my back, I drew her into the crook of my arm. When she tucked her head under my chin, I buried my nose in her hair, inhaling deeply. Her scent carried everything I'd ever need to survive. She ran her slender fingers through the dusting of chest hair circling my nipples, sighing.

"I missed you," she said. "I wish we could stay like this forever."

I tightened my arm around her shoulder, brushing a long strand of her hair from her face.

"I missed you back." It was as if no time had passed since we'd last lain in each other's arms. *Almost no time.*

Meredith ran her hand along my arm, around my thigh, across my tight abs and back up my chest. She giggled when my stomach rumbled. I smiled and kissed the top of her head.

"You hungry?"

"I'm starving. Let's get cleaned up and grab a bite to eat."

She rolled off me toward the edge of the bed. I rolled with her, holding her hand as if it were a lifeline. We walked together into the adjoining en suite where light from the setting sun streamed through the cathedral window, high-lighting the mirrored walls and white marble of the large room. The backdrop only enhanced the outline of her naked body.

Meredith opened the door of the glass shower stall and led me inside. She pulled a lever, and water flowed over us like a warm summer rain. We soaped and stroked each other clean, rejoicing in every curve and hollow of each other's bodies. When we emerged, I used my tongue and a thick black towel on every droplet of moisture clinging to her. The pout of her labia beckoned, and I drew my finger between them. Air escaped my lips, the whisper of a breeze that did little to dissipate the heat of the moment.

Meredith cupped my face in her hands and kissed me with a hunger so raw a shock wave arced through me, pene-trating deep into my core. She dropped her hands to my chest and backed me onto the vanity chair sitting in the corner. Grabbing a towel from a nearby stack, she placed it on the floor and sank to her knees between my legs. The tip of her pink tongue traced a promise of what was to come while she pulled her hair into a loose knot. My penis stood at attention at the thought of her warm, wet mouth.

Using one finger and the viscous pre-cum leaking from my cock, she drew a line on the underside of my throbbing hard-on. She followed the trail of moisture it left, first with her tongue, and then with the same slender finger. She licked and traced until I thought I'd go mad with the craving to bury myself deep in her mouth. I held the sides of her head, eager to slide into her, but she pushed back and looked at me.

"It's my turn now." With a smirk, she grazed the tip of my thick shaft with her lips.

I'd forgotten what it was like with a woman who embraced her oral fixation. Although it didn't seem possible, Meredith went a step further—she devoured my cock as if it were a gourmet treat.

I couldn't help groaning as I watched her magnificent mouth play with my tool. She licked. She sucked. She nibbled. She licked some more. She worked me over until I sat, head thrown back, gasping. Soon, all that existed was her mouth on me. Every time I got close to coming, she backed off just enough to torture me. Then she'd proceed with a greedy ferocity, curling her tongue around my shaft before taking me deep within the recesses of her hot mouth.

My balls were so tight they formed two knots of tension pulling into my pelvis. When I thought I'd die from aching for release, she took one last deep suck and let me explode. I arched back on the chair and roared my total surrender, something I hadn't done for a very long time. I collapsed, spent, making harsh, ragged gasps.

I opened my eyes to find Meredith's fastened on mine, a smug smile on those gorgeous lips. She sat back on her haunches and held my semi-erect cock in her hands, worshipping at the altar of my debauchery. Her lips glistened with my climax, and a look of self-satisfaction settled over her captivating features.

I gathered her onto my lap. I licked and kissed her full lips, reveling in the taste of my sex mingled with the spicy undertones of her sweet breath. A twinge of life shot through my penis as it lay snug under her fleshy ass.

"Enough of that or we'll never get out of here." She playfully shoved herself away from my lap. "Come on. Let's get dressed."

I followed her into the bedroom where I tugged on the clothing I'd unceremoniously dumped on the floor in my haste to reclaim her body. Unbelievably, my erection sprang back to life while I watched her wiggle into jeans and a top. It was going to be a great summer.

2

I sat draped behind the wheel of the car, my white-linen shirt open, emphasizing my flat stomach hugged by a Tshirt over jeans. Although I was an average-looking guy, women admired my body. I rolled my shirtsleeves just the way Meredith liked. Her breath caught as she gazed at me, her fingers brushing through the fine hairs sprinkled across my forearms. She laid her head back against the headrest.

"I love the way your chiseled back rolls into the curves of your nice firm butt." *Good grief! How does a man respond to a comment like that?* Unable to think of anything, I smiled at the compliment.

Everything was happening so fast. A lot can change in three years, and I told myself to slow down. I resisted the part of me that wanted to fold her within me forever. I ignored the tiny voice in my head that kept whispering, *Run, Connor, run.* But somehow, my vow not to get caught under her spell was the furthest thing from my mind whenever she was near.

I turned the key in the ignition, and the engine purred to life.

"Nice car."

"It's a 1971 Porsche 914-6."

"Beautiful." I tapped the accelerator, grinning at the sound of the powerful engine. Although nineteen years old, the car purred as if new. After spending a few minutes learning the lay of the console and adjusting the mirrors, I shifted slightly in the leather bucket seat. In that small movement, I merged with the sports car to become one high-performance unit.

"Where to?" I put my hand on the stick shift and looked over at Meredith, grinning.

Meredith seemed delighted by my enthusiasm. "Are you still a steak-and-potatoes man, or have you cultivated more exotic culinary tastes?"

"I'm still pretty much a meat-and-potatoes kind of guy, but I'm willing to try anything once. Why, what did you have in mind?"

"Do you remember the steak house we went to in Port Elgin?"

"It wasn't a night I'm likely to forget."

Meredith's gaze fastened on the way my hand stroked the gearshift. She'd loved my hands and my tapered fingers. A shiver ran through me as I flashed back to how those fingers had traced her spine and caressed her nipples.

"What's the matter? Are you cold?"

"No, I'm good. I'm remembering. That's all."

Something in her tone drew my attention. Her blue eyes burned, making heat rise through my body. She'd chosen a sleeveless black-silk blouse tied at the waist with the top three buttons undone to show a hint of her bare breasts. A pair of jeans and flats completed the outfit. Meredith chose not to flaunt her sexuality, however, she couldn't resist a bit of enticement. She'd made the right choice.

I put the car into gear and accelerated. The Porsche

coasted past the manicured lawns leading to the long, tree-lined driveway.

"How come you have a race car? Does it belong to your father or something? I asked.

She laughed. "It's not a race car. It's not even very powerful. And no, it doesn't belong to my father. It was a gift. Why? What kind of car do you drive?"

"Whatever I can get my hands on."

By the time we reached the outskirts of Kincardine, I was in my element and drove with confidence. Meredith pressed a button on the sound system, and the music of the Eagles blended with the early summer sounds of the small town. I drummed the steering wheel and hummed along with Don Henley belting out "Hotel California."

Meredith ran her fingers along the side of my face before letting her hand come to rest on my arm. Warmth radiated through her hand, spreading through me like the burn of a fine brandy. I purred with contentment as she traced the contours of my arm with her nails. I did love how it felt having my arm scratched.

I pulled into a parking spot in front of the restaurant and pocketed the keys while I waited for her to get out of the car. Her body was toned and tanned with the proportions of a goddess. She carried herself with an easy grace.

I slid my hand around the back of her neck as we climbed the stairs to the entrance of the steak house. Meredith smiled at me and snuggled into my grasp as I opened the ornate wood and brass door.

"Good evening, madam." The maître d' glanced at me.

"Good evening, Charles," Meredith says.

"Your table is ready. Will anyone else be joining you, this evening?"

"No, there's just the two of us." Meredith's tone would have given General Patton pause.

Charles flushed, looking haughty. "I ask only because the other gentleman was asking after you."

"As I said, it's just us." Her clipped tone ended the discussion.

"Right this way." The *maître d'* led the way through the busy dining room to a private alcove in a back corner of the restaurant. He pulled the inside chair out for Meredith, and I took the other. He shook a napkin and placed it on Meredith's lap before doing the same for me. *Fancy.*

"Your server will be right with you. Is there anything else I can do for you this evening?"

"No, thank you, that will be all, Charles."

Meredith opened her menu before glancing up to see me staring.

"What's the matter?"

"Who's the other gentleman?"

"I haven't the foggiest idea, Connor. Now let's order. I'm famished." Meredith returned her attention to the menu with studied interest, evidently hoping I'd let the question slide. After a moment's hesitation, I did the same.

Just then, a tall, muscular man appeared at our table. Heat colored Meredith's throat and cheeks. *Mystery solved.*

"I see I still make you blush, my *petite amante*. I was hoping to see you here."

"Hello, Ken. Let me introduce you to my *date*. Connor, meet Ken Shantz. Ken, meet Connor McClane."

I started to rise from my chair, hand outstretched. The red-haired man glanced at me with piercing charcoal-gray eyes before returning his gaze to Meredith. I blushed, dropped my hand, and sat.

"I can see that I'll have to wait." Ken's tone made it obvious he was used to getting what he wanted and didn't like to be kept waiting. "I'll see you soon, very soon." He picked up Meredith's hand, kissed the back of it, and left.

"Who . . . was . . . that?"

"Just a man I met at the bar last week."

"He didn't act like someone you just met last week. And what's this about seeing you soon?"

Meredith's lips tightened. She took a deep breath.

"He's doing some business with my guardian that I'm helping with."

Why are you lying?

I could feel her thoughts crawl over me as if she'd spoken aloud—*You're being intrusive.* After a long moment, I sighed.

"I have so much to learn about you." Although I'd spent a lot of time in this woman's bed, I knew little about her.

A pretty, ponytail-swinging, gum-chewing server appeared at the table. "Hi. I'm Candy. Are you ready to order, or do you need a few more minutes?"

"I'm ready to order," Meredith said. "Are you?"

"Sure, I'll have a steak, medium rare, with lots of fried onions and mushrooms." I handed the unopened menu to the server.

"What kind of steak, sir?"

"What kind of steak would you suggest?"

I deferred to her expertise and turned my complete attention on her, enchanting her with one of my full-on grins.

"Th-th-that depends on wh-what you like, sir."

I widened my grin even more. I liked being treated with deference.

"Something tasty and tender." I winked.

Candy opened the menu I handed her, bent it, and placed it in front of me. She pointed to a selection with a bright-red polished index finger. Her massive mammaries burst from the low-cut and very short black dress she wore.

Meredith stifled a sigh—was it jealousy or insecurity rearing its ugly head? *What the hell is it about big breasts that bother other women?* Still peeved by her lying, I decided to play with Meredith, just a little.

How do you say this, Candy?" I pointed to words on the menu.

Candy straightened, wriggled her tightly skirted tush, and announced, "Stake–oh–pose–ray." I looked up in time to see Meredith's eyes roll to the back of her head. No doubt, she had never heard anyone murder *Steak au poivre* quite so badly in the circles she traveled in.

"What does it come with?"

I could feel another mental eye roll.

"It's served with some kind of sauce, those skinny little French fries, and veg," Candy said, standing and shaking down those bosoms.

Meredith couldn't stand it any longer. She smiled sweetly at her. "Usually it comes with a pan sauce made of reduced cognac, heavy cream, drippings, butter, shallots, and Dijon mustard. And those skinny little French fries are called *pommes frites.*"

Candy's face was an interesting shade of red as she stammered, "Uh-uh yeah, th-th-that's it," and fled the table.

"Shit, she didn't take my order. It's so hard to find good help these days."

I looked at Meredith, daring her to challenge me.

"What?" she asked.

"Was that necessary?"

"Was what necessary?"

"Did you have to embarrass the poor girl? She's just trying to do her job."

"Poor girl, my fucking ass. Really, Connor, are you completely oblivious?"

I bit down on the rip-her-face-off comment threatening to race from my mouth. I could sense Meredith counting to ten. I waited, saying nothing.

Finally, she said, "You're right. That was catty. I don't want to spend our first night together being bitchy. Can we start over?"

I smiled and winked.

"Sure, let's start over. It's so good to see you again, Merry. What have you been up to?" I leaned forward in the chair, rested my forearms on the table, and made it seem as if there was no one else in the world but her at that moment. It never ceased to amaze me how much that meant to women and how easy it was to influence their emotions. I could tell from Meredith's smile that she wasn't fooled but appreciated the flattery.

"There's not much to tell. I finished law school, and in the fall, I'll be articling at a large firm on Bay Street in Toronto."

"Very impressive. But what I really care about is who you are, Merry. What have *you* been up to?"

Maybe she'll tell me the truth. Don't push, Con.

"I guess the answer to that is, not much and a lot."

I brushed a lock of her long dark hair back from her face and gave her one of my smiles destined to shoot straight through her heart.

"Let's start with the 'not much' part. Are you seeing anyone?"

"No one specific. Here's the thing, Connor. I'm not looking to get tied up in a relationship right now. Would it matter to you if I was?"

I paused. "Yes. I know it shouldn't, but I think it would." We stared into each other's eyes, saying nothing. The sound of a clearing throat broke our reverie. Candy blushed deep red again as we looked at her.

"Um, Charles said to give th-this to you on the house." She put a bottle of wine in front of me, took Meredith's order, and fled.

"My God, she's got it bad for you."

"I doubt that. I think you've scared her half to death."

We both laughed. I wondered why they'd given us the wine and figured it must be an apology for missing her order. It was clear that Meredith was well known here. She filled each of our glasses with wine, raised her glass to the light, and gazed at the color. I followed suit. The night was turning out to be a good one after all.

3

"Are you still playing around at being a submissive?" I asked, tucking into the steak.

"Boy, you still cut right to the chase. Are you?"

"Am I what? Pursuing the Dominant/submissive lifestyle? That's been next to impossible."

"How so?"

"Why, there's been no one else but you, Merry, that's why." It was everything I could do to keep from smiling. I had worked on the delivery of that line, and the practice paid off.

Meredith choked on the wine she'd sipped and looked at me, stunned. I managed to keep my gaze impassive, as difficult as it was not to smile.

"You're kidding me, right? There's not a chance you haven't been with other women for the past three years. I don't believe it."

"And why not?"

"Because you've learned too damned much since the last time we made love."

"I read a lot," I said, but my ego got the best of me. I broke into a wide grin.

"Bullshit." She grinned back at me.

"You're avoiding my question. Are you still into the Dom/sub lifestyle?"

Meredith busied herself moving the pasta around her plate. I took another bite of my steak without taking my eyes off her. I waited. She fussed with her food and took another sip of her wine. I waited. *Why did she find the question so difficult?*

"Kind of." She kept her gaze on her plate.

"What did you say?" I wanted to be sure that I'd heard the evasion.

"I said, kind of." Her blue eyes were an icy hue when she raised them to meet mine. She had an edge I didn't remember. Was that a silent challenge?

"Why are you being evasive? It's not like this isn't something we'd talked about before. I don't understand why you're getting defensive."

"Evasive? Defensive? You really know how to romance a woman, don't you?"

"I'm sorry. I don't mean to offend. I'm just curious to know more about who you are. Not what you do, who you are. What makes you tick?"

She took a bite of her food and chewed it slowly. Although she still looked at me, her eyes were focused on a thought somewhere deep within her. She took another sip of wine and sighed. I watched, more fascinated than curious. It was unusual, in my experience, for a woman to let her internal struggle show.

"Yes, I'm still exploring the D/s lifestyle. Do you want to know why?"

"Yes, Merry, I do. I want to know everything you're

willing to share with me." A mischievous smile played over her lips.

"Do you want me to tell you a story about my sex life, or would you prefer to experience it for yourself?"

I grinned. The more playful she became, the more at ease I felt. I enjoyed the cat-and-mouse scenario—the tease, the challenge, the goal. To see who would come out on top.

"Both. When can we start?"

Meredith stared at me for another moment and then sat back as the last remnants of tension flowed from her.

"I tell you what, Connor. I'll tell you a story about one of my experiences on the ride back home, and if you're still interested, I'll show you one of my favorite activities."

"Sounds like a plan. Ready to go?"

Meredith laughed, and the sound was music to my soul. I took even greater satisfaction in the realization the game had begun, and I loved the challenge.

"Not so fast. If I'm going to be telling stories, I need to have dessert first. Something hot and sticky and gooey should do the trick."

"I know just the thing." I loved the warm pink blush lighting her face.

"I don't think so. It has to be something on the menu here."

"That's no fun."

"That depends what chair you're sitting in. It's great fun watching you squirm over there. Should I help you with a little foot play?"

Now it was my turn to look uncomfortable, realizing the game just changed and how easily she regained control.

"It's tempting, but no. I'm not into public displays, remember?"

"We'll have to change that," she said. I tensed, and she laughed.

"Relax, Connor. I'm teasing you." She sat back and sipped her wine until Candy arrived with dessert—a gooey chocolate fudge brownie for Meredith and plain old apple pie à la mode for me. Meredith attacked hers with gusto.

"So it sounds as if you're planning on staying a while," she said between bites.

"Yes, actually. I'm in Kincardine for the summer with a friend." I scrubbed my hand through my brown curls.

"A friend?" A sculpted eyebrow arched.

"Yes, a friend. Did I ever tell you about Brian?"

"Oh, you mean your friend who led you into trouble in high school? You're still hanging around with him?"

"That's the one. Brian Patrick Farrell. Irish-Catholic, born trouble, and my best friend. Our high school experiences reinforced an understanding of what friendship is all about. He has my back, and I have his. Most importantly, he accepts me for who I am without question."

"I'm lucky to have a friend like that, too. So what have you been doing since I last saw you, Connor?"

"I finished my undergrad degree. I took a double major in business admin and biology. I start medical school at the University of Toronto in September. That's about it."

Meredith said nothing for a few seconds. Her gaze penetrated right to my core, and a shiver ran through me.

"And what about your sex life?"

"A double major took most of my time, and as I've said, there's only been you, Merry." I grinned at the look crossing her face.

"Okay, I'll take that as an obvious attempt to flatter me, but I'm not buying it."

Our server returned and left the bill in front of me. Meredith rolled her eyes and reached for it. Something about the buxom beauty really got under her skin, but I refused to acknowledge the spiteful little games women play with each other. Meredith placed some cash in the folder and slid it to the edge of the table. She hadn't left a tip, so I dropped a twenty-dollar bill on the table before following Merry from the restaurant.

"Now let's get out of here. I want to hear that story." I drove from the parking lot and headed into the warm summer night.

"As a legal intern, I got assigned to the occasional meet-and-greets necessary when working at one of the big firms. Most were somewhat tedious assignments but were an unavoidable part of the job. It came as a surprise when one of the senior partners from this elite Bay Street firm invited me to an all-expense-paid, private, members nightclub in New Orleans to give a review of an important brief I'd written. I hesitated but was intrigued particularly because the lawyer was a woman, and so few women make it to senior partner in such a prestigious law firm. When they do, it's rare, in my experience, that they're willing to share the limelight with another female colleague.

"I wasn't disappointed in the renowned lush atmosphere and unique culture New Orleans is famous for. They'd booked me a large room in a luxurious hotel where the club was located. After checking in, I went to meet the partner—let's call her Adriana—and check out the meeting room setup. She was waiting for me at the entrance to a large room housing forty to fifty people who had the time and money to indulge in whatever took their interest.

"Adriana was a striking woman, built like a brick shit-house as you guys are so fond of saying. She represented everything I hoped to achieve in my legal career. After we shook hands, she introduced me to her assistant, who was a lesson in contrast to her. He was very good looking, something like you." Meredith smiled at me. I rested my right hand on her thigh.

"You've got my interest. Go on."

"Adriana had a husky, bedroom voice. She told her assistant to bring me a glass of wine, which he did without the slightest hesitation.

"In fact, he seemed prepared to anticipate anything she wanted. I said something to her about the benefit of having such an excellent assistant, and she smiled. I found it odd none of the attendees spoke to me. Adriana, who monopolized my time, assured me everyone was quite enthusiastic about my presentation. After more wine—"

"That's a lot of drinking at what was supposed to be a business meeting."

"If you want to hear this story, Connor, don't interrupt. It breaks my train of thought. Now, where was I?"

Ouch! "Drinking wine."

"Oh yes, after another glass of wine, Adriana introduced me to a round of applause while I stepped onto the platform. Their applause boosted my confidence, and I began speaking. The lights in the room darkened, save for a single floodlight making me the focus of attention. I was nearing the end of my talk when I felt lightheaded. The last thing I remembered was Adriana's assistant holding me up and saying, 'It is hot in here, and I'm sure the wine isn't helping. Not to worry, I'll take you to your room. After a rest, you'll be fine. You're not used to this humidity.'

"I awoke with a start and opened my eyes to the blinding glare of the single floodlight. I'm telling you, Connor, if it was a dream, it was too vivid. I was on the very stage where I'd presented my brief. I tried to speak, but there was some kind of ball in my mouth, held by straps fastened behind my head. I could breathe, but I couldn't talk. I lifted my head and was stunned to find I was lying naked on a platform about the size of a single bed elevated about four feet. Padded cuffs held my arms near my sides. My legs were bent at the knees, and more cuffs at my knees and ankles held them apart."

I went rock hard at the vision of my Merry spread wide for the world to see. I could imagine her nubile body, glistening with a sheen of sweat, moisture building between her legs. *Cool!*

"The now all-too-familiar husky voice said, 'Blindfold her.' The audience broke into applause. Everything went dark when masculine fingers tied a silk scarf over my eyes. I lay helpless and exposed. Adriana whispered in my ear, 'Welcome to our initiation ceremony. Think of it as a test, if you will. You are the preferred candidate, but acceptance to our inner circle is exclusive and requires a certain taste for the esoteric. I wonder if you're up to the challenge.'"

I wondered, too. The bulge in my pants cried for release, and it was everything I could do to keep from squirming. Meredith's soft and seductive voice wasn't helping matters, either.

"'My assistant is very gifted at bringing out the hidden desires that lie deep within. You will learn control. You will enjoy the process. You will experience the pain and pleasure of prolonged levels of excitement. You will resist orgasm until the very end, or I will punish you. Now let us begin.'"

My logical brain kicked in. I raised an eyebrow. "Seriously, Mer? It sounds like you've been reading a lot of erotica."

"Do you want to hear the story or not?"

"Absolutely. I'm just saying."

Meredith inhaled, paused, and continued.

"In a rush of panic, I struggled with the restraints. My screams of protest were muffled by the ball gagging me. True to her word, the stinging slap from a flat leather strap hit my exposed inner thigh, and man, did it hurt. 'Lie still,' she said.

"I'm not sure whether it was the fear of more pain or the

dreadful silence making my helplessness all the more real and frightening, but I stopped struggling. The assistant applied lotion to both of my nipples with what felt like a soft paintbrush. It traced from the outside of my areola to my now erect nipples. The liquid warmed, and my nipples grew even harder, swollen, and full. Someone put clamps on the lip of each labia, and I could feel delicate links of chains lying across my thighs and around my hips. I was wide open and exposed. He painted more liquid on my clitoris. The warmth made my clit painfully swollen. It felt engorged beyond anything I'd ever experienced, hard, like a small erect penis exposed even more because my lips were wide apart.

"I caught a whiff of the assistant's cologne as his fingers encircled my left breast, capturing it in a squeezing grip that extended my nipple to a peak. A wet tongue flicked at the tip, followed by lips sucking hard and long. He sucked each nipple alternately. Although I resisted, overwhelming desire started to replace any thought of being violated."

Meredith paused, shut her eyes, and rested her head on the headrest as though she were reliving the experience. I said nothing and squeezed her thigh, encouraging her to continue.

4

My grip on Meredith's thigh tightened. She slid her arm under mine, placing a hand on my crotch. A rock-hard erection strained against my jeans. Meredith let out a big breath, and I loved that, for a moment, she seemed too distracted to continue with her story.

"I moaned, wanting and needing to be sucked. Hot breath tormented my clit. Then she whispered in my ear, 'Will I let him suck your clit?' Rational thought blew from my mind. The muscles in my body contracted, and a mouth clamped down on the base of my clitoris, rhythmically sucking its length further and further in. As suddenly as it started, he stopped, leaving me gasping, pushing my hips against the restraints, seeking more.

"Adriana got rid of any thought of resistance when she whispered, 'I am going to take the gag off, but you are not allowed to speak unless it is in response to anything I might ask. Don't disappoint me!'

"After she removed the blindfold and gag, she undid the cuffs from the chain holding my arms to my sides, allowing me to move. She paused, staring at me. 'Roll over, ass high in the air, and spread your butt with your hands.' I hesitated and felt a painful slap of leather on my upper thighs. 'Now.' I moved onto my knees and grabbed each of my cheeks. 'Good. Now pull each cheek apart so we can see that sweet little pucker of yours.'"

Holy shit. This just keeps getting better and better. I was going to burst right out of my jeans. Meredith was so engrossed in her story, she seemed oblivious to my discomfort.

"As I held my cheeks apart, she applied a warm lubricant before inserting first one, then two fingers. My muscles clamped down on her fingers. It was the first time anyone had ever penetrated my ass, and intense pleasure replaced discomfort as she worked my hole. I squirmed, against my will, wanting more. Still, she took her time, massaging me with her fingers until my sphincter relaxed. She inserted a lubricated probe inch by inch until it was buried inside me. 'Are you ready for more?' All I could do was moan loudly—there was no denying my desire. The assistant's wet fingers slid into my dripping cunt, stopping when they reached the juncture of his hand. Long, slow strokes from the tip to the base of the fingers gradually increased in urgency.

"'Do you want to come? Do you want me to let him fuck you hard and deep?'

"'Yes,' I gasped. She slapped my ass.

"'Good. I like it when you beg. Now say please.'

"'Please,' I moaned. A thick, rigid cock replaced the fingers. I've never felt so full with everything stimulated at once. My hips thrust upward, taking on a life of their own. I lost control. Nothing existed except my need to come. I would beg for release if necessary. Just when I thought I couldn't take it anymore, Adriana said, 'Fuck her hard and deep the way she wants.'"

Yes, the way I want.

"Immediately the assistant complied, thrusting harder

and deeper again and again. I heard an animalistic scream when I came, and I was shocked to realize it came from me. My body shook with violent spasms."

The image of Meredith writhing on that stage overwhelmed my every thought. I desperately held on to any sense of control, knowing I was on the verge of losing it.

"I must have passed out because the next thing I remember was waking in my room at the hotel. Usually, I'm very analytical, but this was different. I couldn't help thinking I should have resisted more. On the other hand, the whole experience excited me in ways I never thought possible. Perhaps I wasn't ready to know what lay hidden inside me. I showered, packed, checked out, and took the next flight home. I knew I was unusually tired and sore, but I've never admitted experiencing anything more than bad wine and dreams."

By this time, I was parked in front of the estate, my head thrown back against the headrest, eyes closed, listening. I took slow, measured breaths, grateful the pulse in my engorged cock beneath Meredith's hand was the only obvious indication the story affected me. She got out of the car, opened my door, and took me by the hand. I followed, taking deep mental breaths, too. This wouldn't be a good time for a premature ejaculation, that's for sure. She led me around the side of the house onto the starlit patio, stopping beside a cushioned, molded chaise.

Meredith's eyes were intense with desire in the light of the full moon. She slid her fingers under my shirt and inched it over my well-formed biceps. Shivers of excitement seemed to run through her as her fingers brushed the fine silky hair on my forearms. She let the shirt drop onto the granite patio stones and undid my jeans. Each movement of this slow dance of seduction sent a corresponding shiver through me.

She tugged on my Tshirt, and I raised my arms, allowing her to pull it over my head. It joined the shirt on the patio.

Meredith placed her hand on a powerful hard-on that, restrained by my briefs, bulged through the open zipper of my jeans. I watched with delight as passion flared in her eyes.

"I believe you liked my story," she said.

Eyes never leaving mine, she removed her black-silk blouse and jeans one piece at a time as if performing a dance to a smooth, smoky blues tune only she could hear. Her nipples stood at attention, and the scent of her arousal caused a visceral reaction within me.

She stepped toward me, inhaling deeply. She worked my jeans and briefs over my legs and paused to study my body. Normally, this was something that made me uncomfortable, but I basked in the pleasure she displayed. She licked a finger and ran it along the length of my shaft.

"You are perfection." Standing, she blew a light breath past my ear. "The model used for Michelangelo's David."

My cock stood at attention, inviting her to envelop it in her warmth, and she wrapped her hand around it as if she couldn't wait any longer to have it fill her.

Her teeth tore the wrapper from the condom she rolled over me. She shoved me onto the chaise lounge. Straddling me, she once again wrapped her hand around my pulsing cock, guiding me into her. She eased onto me, and heat seared through me as I filled her.

Our eyes remained locked, and the fire in hers excited me. It was as if she'd found a place to call home after a long journey. She was made for me, and I completed her. Joy spread through me as she rode me. I was ready to burst, but I kept my breathing even and matched to hers. I didn't move, accepting her need to pleasure herself with me—actually, I couldn't move or I would have exploded. She kept her rhythm slow, seeming to match my control. Her tight pussy clenched with each stroke. I was drowning in lust.

When I couldn't take it anymore, I grabbed her ass and took control of the rhythm. Her eyelids started to close. I tightened my grip on her toned cheeks. "Look at me," I whispered.

Her lids flew open, eyes searing mine with her unblinking, smoldering gaze. I increased the rhythm and thrust into her again and again. The pleasure was so intense I thought I'd erupt. Her eyes drifted shut.

I squeezed her ass, hard, holding her suspended until she opened them again. I continued, relentlessly, until she was trembling with the urge for release. Yet I kept her on the edge of the precipice. Meredith started to moan. She dug her nails into my shoulders, fighting to take the control from me, but she was no match for my strength. I held her, suspended, one last time, and plunged into her as the force of my orgasm shot through her. With a loud moan, she collapsed onto my chest.

We held each other, unmoving, prolonging the moment and letting the night air cool our passion-heated skin.

"Come to bed with me," she said.

I stayed at the beach house with her for the next two weeks. Apart from my summer job, we spent every moment together. I wasn't sure what came over me. It wasn't like me to get involved with my lovers. Why did Meredith have such power? What made her different from the others?

On my days off, I took her to see my childhood haunts. She wanted to know everything about me, which was awkward and flattering at the same time. Yet she had a way of knocking down the walls we all hide behind.

We toured the shores of Lake Huron, visiting Wiarton and Colpoy's Bay. On one such day, energized by a morning quickie, we decided to head over to Wasaga Beach to hang out on the boardwalk and mingle with the tourists. Waves of heat radiated from the pavement and drifted into the clear, brilliant sky.

Meredith wore a revealing turquoise bikini top and cutoff jeans, and it was all I could do to keep my hands off her. I was the kid in the proverbial candy store, but I contented myself by playing with the fine hairs on the back of her neck. She'd tossed off her sandals and sat with her feet on the dashboard of the Porsche.

"Do you remember the story you told me my first night back?"

Meredith turned her head toward me, and I glanced back. I was thankful for the sunglasses shielding my eyes.

"Yes, I remember. Why?"

"Was it a true story?"

"What do you think?"

"I don't know, Merry. That's why I'm asking." I kept my voice neutral.

"Would you think any differently of me if it were true?"

I could feel Meredith's gaze trained on me through her sunglasses. I took a moment and thought. "I have to admit I'm a little jealous when I think of someone else fucking you. But, no, ultimately, it wouldn't or shouldn't make a difference."

"Does the thought excite you?"

Again, I took a moment before answering. "That's a hard question to answer. To be completely honest, the concept excites me. You know that from what happened after you told me the story. Would watching someone fuck you for real excite me? I really don't think I can answer that. Part of me thinks it would, but the selfish part of me thinks it's revolting. What would you think of me fucking someone else?"

Meredith paused before answering. The intent of my question struck home. If there was a time to be open with me, this was it.

Are you fucking someone else?

She gazed out of her window for several minutes as if the passing countryside held the answers. Finally, she said, "Yes, I think it would bother me and excite me, and I don't know which would be worse. But if you ordered me to, I think I would be excited to watch."

"Do you do everything you're ordered to do?"

"If the order comes from my Master, I do." I could barely hear her.

"Your *Master*. And just who is your Master?" My tone held the edge of finely honed steel.

"Maybe we shouldn't get into this right now, Connor. I've been honest with you about being a submissive, and you've never been curious about it before. Are you sure you're ready to know?"

"For fuck's sake, Meredith! Don't put this on me. You've had plenty of opportunity to tell me if there's another man in your life. A lie by omission is still a lie. Fuck!" I took my hand from the back of her head and smacked the steering wheel, hard. "Fuck!" Even though Meredith hadn't moved, I felt her withdraw from me. *You and your damned temper, Connor.*

We rode in silence a while longer. I let out a long sigh. "I'm sorry. I lost my temper. I do want to know who you are no matter what that means to me. I'd rather know the truth than live a lie."

"Me too, Connor, but that Scorpio temper of yours is getting the better of you, and I'm not willing to share my lifestyle if you're not ready to accept it."

"I'll do my best. However, even you've got to admit if the shoe was on the other foot, you'd be upset. Wouldn't you?"

"Yes, I would. I already admitted that. Although they are not mutually exclusive, it is hard to separate love from lust, and yet people do it all the time."

Love? Don't go there, Connor.

"Okay, can we start over, please? Do you have a Master?"

"Not right now, but I've had a couple of Masters before and since I first met you."

I glanced at her, eyebrows raising. "What do you mean by before and since you met me? You were twenty-one when we met, right? You mean you've been living this lifestyle, as you call it, since you were a kid?"

"Not a kid, exactly. I'd started my training a couple of months before I met you that summer."

"How did you meet these Masters? Were they even men?"

The edges of Meredith's mouth quirked as my curiosity overcame my emotional turmoil.

"Yes, they were men. Would you feel any better about it if it was a woman?"

I grinned. "Maybe. It would be a hell of a lot easier to fantasize about, that's for sure. How did you meet them?"

"One was a friend of Brett's, and one I met at a club."

"A friend of Brett Sandvine's?" Incredulity raised the pitch of my voice. "You mean the guy who owns the estate, that Brett?"

"Yes, that Brett." Look, do you want to hear the story, or what?"

"Okay, okay. I'll shut up and listen." I returned to stroking the back of her neck, and she relaxed in her seat.

"I'm an only child, and I grew up in a loving household. My parents were very much in love, and as I later found out, hugely into the Dom/sub thing.

"They had a special room in the house they kept locked.

They called it their playroom and told me it was for adult games. Sometime when I was around thirteen or fourteen, I got curious about it, so I watched whenever they went into it. They stayed for hours, and sometimes I heard sounds that made me more curious than ever.

"My dad usually carried the key, but once he forgot it. My mom went back to their bedroom for it, so I knew they kept it in there. When they were away on a trip, I found the key and went in. Even though I'd just started fooling around with boys, I knew enough to figure out it was a sex playroom, and I was more excited than shocked to see their toys."

"What kinds of toys?" She had my full attention.

"A whipping post, and dildos, and whips, and nipple clamps, and gags, a bunch of bottles of lubricant, and lots of restraints."

"Wow, wasn't it kind of weird thinking of your parents using that stuff?"

"Here's the thing, Connor. I didn't find it weird. It fascinated me, and I wanted to try the stuff. Part of me felt as if I belonged there. I fantasized about it all the time when I masturbated. Then, when I was sixteen, my parents were killed in a boating accident. I can't even describe the pain. It's still hard to talk about. I was devastated, as you can well imagine, and sex was the only thing that turned off the anguish.

"So I started looking for guys who were willing to experiment, and I started hanging out with an older and rougher crowd. Most of the guys had no idea about what it meant to be a Dominant. They were aggressive, and a couple of them hurt me, but overall, I came to realize I liked being forced.

"One of them took me to a BDSM club and made me strip in front of everyone and whipped me. If it hadn't been for Brett, he might have hurt me badly. Brett knew my parents through the lifestyle and was appointed my guardian when they died. He rescued me. After talking with me for a while, he realized I was a submissive. He explained that the men I was with weren't Dominants. They were predators. I was young and defiant, and I insisted I was going to explore and would be fine. He knew some of these men and what they were capable of, and he wanted to protect me. So he offered to find me a Dom, and being driven by adolescent hormones, I agreed. After all, I was eager to experiment.

"So what about Brett?" I paused. "Do you love him?"

"He means a great deal to me, and yes, I love him for many reasons. He's my guardian and my mentor. He's been very good for me, and he'll always have a special place deep in my heart. As for the other men, they're part of my past—the operative word being *past*. Can you live with that?"

"I don't know. I think so. I don't know how I'm feeling right now, although since we're being open and honest, I must admit a part of me is excited by this. You've given me a lot to think about. Thanks for trusting me." I pulled the car into a parking spot a block away from the lake and put it in park.

"I think you should tell me more about being a submissive."

"Yes, I should," she laughed.

We strolled to the beach hand in hand.

5

"You look like the cat that ate the canary," Brian said. He settled into the lounger beside mine. "I was wondering if I'd ever see you again."

I smiled, pushed my sunglasses up, and leaned my head back. I loved the sun almost as much as I loved sex and spent every possible moment soaking up its rays. I was one of the lucky ones who tanned from golden brown to a deep bronze as the summer flew by.

"I've been busy. What have you been up to?"

Brian snorted. "Busy. Is that what you call it? You are the master of understatement."

I turned my head toward him, my smile broadening. "This from the master of the single *entendre*." I liked Brian's shoot-from-the-hip, take-no-prisoners attitude. "I repeat, what have you been up to?"

"I guess that's as close as I'm going to get to hearing about how things are going with this mystery woman. I've been up to the usual—work, wine, women, and song. Maybe you should join me for a change."

"Anyone interesting I should hear about?"

"You know, Con, I don't know why you think I should spill my guts when you never tell me a thing about what's going on in your life."

"Because you love to talk, and I like to listen. And, besides, I tell you lots of things about my life. More than I tell anyone else." I ran a finger through the dew weeping on my beer before taking a swig of it.

"And that's supposed to appease me?"

I sighed, somewhat amused and somewhat exasperated. Brian was relentless when he had something on his mind. "What do you want to know?"

"Let's see. I haven't seen hide nor hair of you for a couple of weeks now. I figure if you've given up on your usual playboy behavior, this must be someone special. Tell me about her."

"What playboy behavior? I hardly think you can call me a playboy."

"Don't go there, Con. Spill."

"Okay, okay. Remember me telling you about the woman I met when I spent the summer here three years ago?"

"You mean the hot one with the hot sports car?"

"You sure have a way with words, Bri. Yes, that's the one."

"I call them like I see them. You know that. So spill. Her name was Mary or something, wasn't it?"

I gazed toward the lake for a few minutes. Brian waited, his fingers tapping their usual staccato rhythm on the arm of his lawn chair. He knew better than to interrupt me if he wanted to hear more. As I thought about Meredith, a feeling I couldn't put my finger on washed over me, like the reverent awe you get when you walk into a cathedral. Despite my best intentions, I was falling for this woman, and falling hard.

"Her name is Meredith, and she's the most amazing woman I've ever met, Bri. Nothing like the simpering idiots

I've met at university. She's beautiful, intelligent, strong, mysterious, elegant, and she's a lawyer."

"So she'll be rich, too. You've got to be the luckiest son of a bitch I know. You forgot to mention sexy."

I grinned. "That goes without saying."

"If your women didn't tell me what a great lay you were, I might think you were a monk."

"All what women? I want names, Bri. Give me names." We laughed and took another swig of beer.

"I'm thinking this woman has her claws into you so deep the Connor I know might be losing himself."

I need this woman to need me, to want me. The thought was a flame bursting into life, frightening me and invigorating me. I shook it off, but one thought led to another, and I started a journey down memory lane.

Brian's comment took me back to that summer three years ago when I first met Meredith. She took my virginity and taught me what it was to be a man. It was the summer of my eighteenth year. My father arranged for me to work for a friend delivering prescriptions in the small beach town of Kincardine in the hope the experience would bring me out of my shell before I headed off to university. Shy and inhibited, I projected an air of arrogance people interpreted as aloofness. In fact, I was extremely uncomfortable in my own skin. Slim, shy, and just leaving the awkward stage, I had few friends, Brian being the notable exception.

We had been friends since childhood. I admired his brash confidence, resulting in a different girl on his arm every other week. An exaggeration? Maybe. But it sure seemed that way. He never hesitated to point out I had better start dating or people would think I didn't like girls. I would laugh, knowing in truth, the female form fascinated me, always had and always would. My hands itched to touch the voluptuous breasts and hips and nether parts of the women spread-eagled across the glossy pages of what everyone referred to as girlie magazines. Instead, I caressed my cock and jerked off as fast and as often as I could. What I lacked in finesse, I made up for with enthusiasm. I loved the intense body high that came with each ejaculation, and it became my drug of choice.

I would have liked nothing better than to touch the girls I went to school with, but that would have required talking to them. I didn't want to talk, and I didn't want to date—I wanted to fondle. If that made me some kind of nice-guy chauvinist, then so be it. When girls talked to me, and plenty of them did, I thought about touching their breasts and their private parts, and my cock would spring to attention, causing me to flee in embarrassment. So when I wasn't with Brian, I spent time alone. Unsure what to do with me, my parents decided to ship me off to Kincardine for the summer with the hope a summer job at my Uncle Moe's pharmacy would cure me of what they called *social anxiety*.

It was one of those perfect summer days, clear and hot with the hint of a breeze. I rode my bike to the mansion on the edge of town to make the final delivery of the day. The gates stood open, and I followed the long shady lane to the house. I rang the doorbell several times, but no one answered. I resisted the urge to hammer on the door. I couldn't wait to be done for the day so I could head down to the lake, put on my sunglasses, and watch the beach babes as their soft tits bounced and jiggled in their bikinis.

When there'd been no answer at the door, I'd wandered around the back of the house and stared at the expanse of private beach skirting the magnificent Lake Huron. Lost in my own private world, I nearly jumped out of my skin when a voice behind me said, "Boo."

I jumped and almost fell into the most gorgeous woman I'd ever seen. She wore nothing but a string bikini on her five-foot, eight-inch frame. Her sapphire-blue eyes looked into mine, reminding me of the husky that had been my childhood companion. With a toss of her hip-length curls, Meredith introduced herself and offered me a drink of lemonade. She'd focused her attention on me the way no one ever had, and we'd chatted far into the evening. I was comfortable around her. Maybe it was the unpretentious ease with which she carried herself or the way she guided the conversation, but I could have talked with her forever. She was visiting for the summer while taking a break from her university studies. She'd made me feel important. She'd made me feel like a man.

She'd spread her legs and invited me into her. Okay, truth be told, that's not exactly how it happened, but so began a lifetime of sinful sex. I smiled at my naïveté, remembering how she taught me to make love to a woman, how to take my time and explore my sexuality. She'd taught me control while letting me experience what I'd thought were my wildest fantasies with her. When I'd thought I'd gone too far, she'd ask for more. The two months sped by. Even though I knew she'd be going off to university to study law, I'd fallen for her. I'd grown moodier and moodier as the time to go home grew nearer, wondering whether I'd ever see her again.

When she'd dropped me off that last day, I'd leaned into the window of her car while she encouraged me to hone my newfound skill with girls my own age. I'd assured her I'd never be satisfied with the girlish games they played. But she'd told me I'd better practice what she'd taught me if I was going to be ready for what she had in store. She expected to hear updates when I visited her in Toronto. She'd revved the engine of her vintage red Porsche, and with a wink, she drove away.

The experience with Meredith had left me with little desire to focus on the mundane studies of that first year of university. She, however, focused on her studies. Law isn't a program of study, it's a vocation, and Meredith submerged herself in it. We snuck in as many visits and phone calls as we could, but they became fewer and farther between. Then she accepted a scholarship and went off to France.

With Brian's encouragement, I developed a social life. He introduced me to some musicians he'd met. We joined them and formed a band with Brian on drums and me as lead singer. Without any effort on my part, we captured the attention of the popular crowd, and they welcomed us. He thought my exceptional good looks and sexual prowess made me a target, a chick magnet, as he called it. He thought I could have any girl of my choosing. He said it with a sense of wonder. I'd been blessed with good genes and kept my body lean and hard. But when I looked in the mirror, an ordinary guy looked back at me, kind of average, really. I didn't spend a lot of time dwelling on the why of it all; I simply enjoyed my good fortune.

Although I missed Merry, I reminded myself I was following through with her wishes. However, the pain consuming me when she left was enough to convince me the joy of love was highly overrated. I decided I'd mistaken my first crush for love. I took care not to become involved in an ongoing relationship, but graciously accepted those who offered to spread their legs, no strings attached. All the while, I fantasized about Meredith and how she lost herself in her lust.

"So when am I going to meet this marvel?" Brian interrupted, pulling me back from my thoughts.

"We're going out for dinner on Friday night. If you know a girl who could actually carry on a conversation, you might want to join us."

"Yeah, yeah, that's just what I look for with the ladies.

Besides, how can you bear not seeing her for two whole days? I'm shocked."

"Fuck off, Bri," I said, laughing. "She has some business to take care of."

"Business? Sounds mysterious. What kind of business?" Brian was a nosey bugger. It must be the small town in him.

"So what have you been doing lately? Met anyone special?"

"Okay, I get it. Time to change the subject. You know my motto, Con. Play the field. I've met quite a few special ladies. In fact, I'm going to meet more of them tomorrow night at the main beach bonfire. Want to tag along?"

"I don't think so. I'll hang out here and have a quiet night."

"Oh, come on. I thought this was going to be our last chance to sow our wild oats together before you're immersed in medical school. I thought you weren't going to get involved. I thought you were going to take it as it comes. What was all that, talk? Come on, man. Don't be such a stick in the mud. Maybe you should ask this girl for permission."

I laughed at Brian's intensity and refused to take the bait. He could be so dramatic.

"Okay, okay. I'll come. I won't be hooking up with anyone, but I could use the distraction."

"Let me guess. You're going to do your usual sit back and take in the action thing. No wonder people think you're a snob."

"I'm not a snob. I need to know what I'm getting into before jumping in with both feet like you do."

"I don't jump in—I dive in. Life's too short to sit on the sidelines, I always say."

"And at the rate you dive in, your life will be shorter."

"Live hard and fast, that's my other motto. I'm not waiting for it to come to me, that's for sure. I don't know how you have any fun, Con." Brian stood, drained his beer, and lifted his helmet from the patio table. "Time for work. I'll see you later."

After a few minutes, I heard the hum of his Honda Gold Wing roaring down the beach road. I shook my head. One of these days, Brian was going to kill himself on that thing. A small part of me wished I could live the carefree lifestyle that suited him so well. But I wanted to know where I was going and how I was going to get there. I was beginning to realize I liked to be the one calling the shots.

I spent the rest of the afternoon soaking up the sun. Although it looked as if I was watching the activity on the beach from the shelter of my sunglasses, my gaze was locked on the horizon of my own thoughts. Brian was right. I preferred to be on the outside looking in. Sometimes I surprised myself and enjoyed taking complete control of a situation. This happened rarely, and only when I was comfortable. Usually, I preferred to observe myself as much as I did my surroundings.

I wasn't sure how I felt about Meredith. Even though she struck an emotional chord deep within me, one that no other woman had, I wasn't sure what those feelings were. Was it just another summer fling or was I falling in love with her? And what was she hiding from me? I detested any kind of emotional turmoil and tended to shut the door firmly on any hint of it. Yet I couldn't deny that every time I thought about Meredith, that door opened wider and wider.

Longing surged through me. It had been only a few hours, but I couldn't stop thinking about her. I hoped Meredith's business meeting would end early and we'd be together again tomorrow.

Maybe I shouldn't have accepted Bri's offer to party. Or is a party what I need?

6

I woke early the next morning, which was unusual for me. I yearned to see Meredith and couldn't get back to sleep. I slipped into a pair of cutoff jeans, a shirt, and deck shoes and grabbed a quick shave. Brian was passed out cold in the other bedroom. I was taking my life in my hands, but I shook him awake anyway.

"What the fuck," he snorted. The alcohol fumes rising from the bed almost knocked me cold. *Typical Bri. I should have known.*

"Sorry to wake you, Bri. I need to borrow your bike. Okay?"

"Yeah, whatever." He was snoring before I turned around. I rooted in the jeans he'd dropped on the floor. No keys. Next, I tried the leather jacket he'd thrown near the front door. Eureka. I shrugged on the jacket and helmet before heading out.

The beauty of that summer morning took my breath away. Dew glistened on the wildflowers lining the deserted beach road as I cruised along. Meredith would be so surprised when I snuggled into bed with her. A distinctive bulge formed in my pants as I thought of the things I'd do for her. I was determined to make her one happy woman.

I cut the engine at the end of the drive and walked the bike to the front door. As expected, Meredith left the patio doors open, and I slipped inside, and crept noiselessly to her room. She lay sleeping, covered by a sheer wrap she wore, and in the early morning light, I could tell it was all that separated her from the breeze off the lake rippling her drapes. Taut nipples standing out from their soft contour accentuated her ample upturned breasts. A tapered waistline met the swell of her hips, tantalizing me to imagine her hidden sex.

I crawled into bed with her. She stirred when I dropped a light kiss across those voluptuous lips, and a big smile greeted me when she opened her eyes.

"Well, well, this is a surprise. To what do I owe this honor?" Her voice was husky with sleep. "I didn't think I was going to see you until tomorrow."

"I wanted to see you." My gaze drifted down her body. "You do realize how your wrap leaves little to the imagination?"

"I think the better question is do *you* like what you see?"

"Very much."

"Well, then, Mr. Connor McClane, maybe we should do something about that."

As I reached to take her into my arms, she held up her hand, stopping me. She pulled me to my feet. I was perfectly still while she unbuttoned my shirt and inched it off my body. She ran her fingers through the sprinkle of hair dusting my chest and undressed me piece by piece until I stood naked in front of her. She admired the view before pulling a condom from the bedside table and rolling it on my throbbing erection.

She's working me like a top. I loved every second of it.

Meredith dropped the sheer wrap to the carpeted floor. Her lips parted and met mine with a shared hunger. Our bodies molded together while our tongues moved in a well-rehearsed dance. Hands, uninhibited in their frenzy, teased every response to a fever pitch.

Panting, I tossed the large throw cushion from the foot of the bed to the floor. My cock was hard as granite, demanding relief. I lifted Meredith and laid her on the plush pillow, elevating her hips. She threw her head back, arched her back, and spread her legs in invitation. I knelt and thrust my cock into her wetness. Rapture shot through me as her warm cunt enveloped me. She responded by wrapping her legs around my torso, pulling me even deeper into her. Each thrust increased the urgency that became a desperate need for physical release. There was none of the subtlety of making love. Oh no. This was an adrenaline junkie's dream, and I lost myself in it.

Then, for reasons I couldn't explain, something changed. Maybe it happened when I looked into her eyes and recognized pure lust. Maybe it was my desire to prolong the moment. Whatever the reason, I wanted more. It would have been easy to give in to everything my body begged for. Too easy! But I loved watching this woman becoming lost in her sexuality. It was the most beautiful thing I could imagine. It ruined me for anything less.

I pushed the full length of my engorged cock into her and stopped. Extending my arms, I raised my upper torso. My only thought was to watch the expression of her need. Her eyes opened wide in an expression that could be interpreted only as anguish. I savored the moment for as long as I could before slowly sliding my cock out of her until I reached the entrance of her glistening cunt.

As her hips thrust forward in a desperate attempt not to lose me, I slid back into her. Each time I penetrated her, I plunged harder and faster, and Meredith moaned louder and longer. I groaned with the effort of holding back my orgasm. Soon, her body started to tremble. I grasped her breasts with each hand, gently squeezing while my thumb and index finger pinched her nipples. Meredith's head rocked from side to side, and in a desperate voice, she begged me, "Please, please, now, please now, please, please!"

I didn't have to be told what *please* meant. I thrust into her hard and fast. Meredith went rigid and exploded in violent spasms, screaming expletives into the warm summer morning. Watching her in the throes of her climax was pure ecstasy, and I prolonged the moment for as long as I could before finally coming undone. We remained tangled, enjoying the moment. I stayed inside her long after our breathing returned to normal. Only then did I whisper in her ear, "I think I want to know everything about you."

We soon drifted off into sleep. I woke a while later, certain I'd heard a helicopter. I reached for her. She was gone. Pausing, I listened, shocked to hear a man's voice, so I pulled on my shorts and followed the sound to the kitchen. I stopped in the hall out of sight. Meredith sat with her back to me on one of the barstools opposite a long, lean figure leaning against the marble countertop, cup of coffee in hand. I stood poised to flee if his head moved my way.

"I didn't expect to see you until tonight," Meredith said.

"I see your Master, Connor McClane, has resurfaced." Golden lashes shielded blue eyes twinkling with humor and belied the scrutiny he gave her.

I flushed with embarrassment.

"He's not my Master. And how do you know it's Connor?" Even I knew it was a stupid question to ask. Although Meredith mentioned Brett only in passing, you could tell by looking at the man very little got past him. By reputation, he knew what was happening usually before it happened. That was one of the traits attributed to his success and wealth. He probably knew what I'd been doing every minute of my time since that first summer. He was the kind of man who had his finger on the pulse of everything and everyone touching his world.

"No need to get defensive. I thought I should check in and see how you're doing, and I see you're doing just fine. And tonight's your scene with Ken at the club."

Scene with Ken at the club. What the fuck does that mean?

Meredith lowered her head and took a sip of her coffee.

"Having second thoughts? He's new and handsome, but comfort and trust will encourage you to let go. Perhaps . . ." Brett's tenor voice interrupted her thoughts.

Meredith looked up.

"You always could read me like a book. I guess you could say I'm having second, third, fourth, and fifth thoughts. I don't know what I feel, but Ken's not the problem, it's Connor. When he came back, it was as if a magnet drew us together. When I'm with him, I'm happy and I want to spend every minute with him. But there's still a part of me that misses the sessions at the club and needs a Master. I believe Connor could make a great Master one day, but everything D/s is new to him. I'm so confused." She drew in a deep breath. Brett studied her for a moment.

"You haven't told him about your extracurricular activities." It was more a statement than a question. Meredith looked down at her cup again.

"A little, not all."

"And why is that?"

For a long while, Meredith said nothing. Warmth radiated from his eyes as they examined her.

"Because I think he's too young and inexperienced to handle it."

Too young. Fuck!

"And?"

"Because I'm afraid of what he'll think of me if he knows the whole truth. And because I'm afraid he won't be able to embrace my lifestyle and accept what I can give."

"You may be underestimating the lad. One thing I do know—it's better for you to tell him than for him to find out another way."

The buzz of helicopter rotors roared to life on the landing pad at the edge of the property.

"Are you leaving already? You just got here. What about tonight?" Alarm tinged the usual melody of her voice.

"Yes, I'm leaving. I've been called to an emergency meeting. If I don't make it back, you'll be fine. Greg will keep an eye out for you. I've arranged for him to pick you up at the yacht club at nine at my slip." Brett placed his cup on the side of the sink. He walked to where Meredith sat on the barstool and lifted her chin with his index finger. A faint smile touched his lips.

"You've come so far, Grasshopper. You will always be my perfect student, and you know I adore you."

He dropped a gentle kiss on her forehead.

"Be true to yourself," he whispered. Then he was gone.

Moving as fast as I could without making a sound, I ran back to the bedroom and paused for a moment to collect my thoughts. Anger warred with the logical part of my brain. *Don't leap to conclusions, Connor. Find out what's going on first.* I dropped my shorts and lay, feigning sleep.

"Wakey, wakey, sleepyhead." Meredith held out a cup of steaming coffee. "Too bad you didn't wake a few minutes sooner. You just missed Brett, and I'd have loved for you to meet him."

Some of my tension eased. "He mustn't have been here long." I yawned and stretched before taking the cup.

"No, not long at all. I think he intended to stay longer, but he got called away to an urgent meeting." She had dressed my coffee the way I liked it—double, double.

"Come on. Get dressed and come down to the kitchen. I'll cook some breakfast for us."

I dressed, took a few sips of the hot coffee, adjusted my thoughts, and followed her to the kitchen. How could I bring up the subject of this scening business?

"So, Merry, my friend Brian wants me to join him for a party tonight, and I'm hoping you can come with me."

"You know I have some business to attend to. I told you that."

"I know, but how long can a business meeting take? I'm sure it won't be too late and we can go after you're done."

"Look, Connor, I can't explain now. I have no idea when the meeting will end and expect it will be late. Can you trust me on this for now, and we can talk about it later? I'll know more after I have the meeting."

At that moment, the phone rang.

"Give me a minute. I'll be right back." Meredith ran for the phone in the next room.

"Hi, Asha. I'm glad you called. How's it going?" Her voice was low, and I strained to hear her.

"Yes, I'm still coming tonight. Pun intended." Meredith laughed and paused for a moment, listening.

"Cool. Have you found out anything more about Ken? All I know is he's a hunk and requested me. You know, I ran into him a couple of weeks ago. He seemed eager."

More silence.

"Nothing. I was with Connor, so it was a brief exchange. But let me tell you, Ash, there sure is something about him."

Silence.

"Not this time, Ash. He just left. He had an urgent business meeting. It was weird, really. He was here when I woke up and talked to me for a while then off he went."

Pause.

"A little. He told me not to worry because Greg would look out for me." She laughed again, presumably at something this Asha was saying on the other end of the line.

"Ash, you have a one-track mind. See you tonight." She hung up the receiver and came back into the kitchen.

"Who was that?"

"That was my best friend, Asha Lamb. Haven't I told you about her?"

I shook my head and took another sip.

"We are kindred spirits. We met the same summer you slipped into my life."

"And who are Ken and Greg?" I struggled to keep the edge from my voice.

"Greg Sinclair is Brett's security chief, and Ken is the man you met at the restaurant your first night back, remember? Asha works with them, and she wondered about the agenda for tonight's meeting."

Why are you lying to me?

Anger flared through me with the sizzle of a red-hot brand meeting flesh. "Do you think I'm a damned idiot?"

She looked at me with shock and doubt.

"Of course not, Connor. What makes you say that?"

"I overheard most of your conversation with Asha, and it didn't sound like any kind of business talk to me."

"So now you're calling me a liar?"

"No, I'm saying I think there's something you're not telling me. This doesn't add up."

"Neither does this interrogation of yours. I have no idea what's gotten into you."

"I detest being lied to—that's what's gotten into me." I slammed the cup down with such force coffee splashed onto the marble countertop.

"I'm not lying to you." Her eyes looked silver from the

sheen of her tears. "I told you I'd explain later. If that's not good enough for you, then—"

I didn't wait for her to answer. I turned and walked out. I regretted it even before the door slammed behind me.

Dammit! Cool move, Connor.

I really had to get a grip on my emotions.

7

"Slow down," I said as Brian two-wheeled his shiny black Camaro into the parking lot of the yacht club.

"Would you quit being such a nervous Nelly, Con? Besides, you know I like my cars and bikes fast and my women faster—"

"Stop the car. There she is." I rolled down the tinted window and leaned my head out. A cacophony greeted me. Seagulls squawked, waves crashed, and tourists squabbled about the inanities of holiday life. Fresh-cut fries and the myriad of smells from the nearby fish shack assaulted my senses.

We sat idling in the humid evening air. Meredith stood beside a large yacht. A silver Lincoln Town Car pulled up in front of her, and she walked toward a tall, dark-haired man holding open the passenger door. My mood plummeted to the depths of Lake Huron. Meredith smiled at him and exchanged a few words before getting into the car. He closed her door and walked around the front of the car with confidence. He didn't get in so much as fold into the driver's side and drove off. Brian put the Camaro in gear and swung out after him.

"So, you're sure you want to go through with this?"

"Yes." It was all I could do to choke out the word. I couldn't believe I'd let him talk me into this, but I had to know the truth.

"Okay. Here we go."

We hit the highway, and Brian maneuvered his car a couple of cars behind the silver sedan. He started to whistle as he followed at a steady pace.

"You're enjoying this, aren't you?" My voice matched the black thunderclouds shadowing my face. I tried to keep a handle on my hair-trigger temper, but I was losing the battle.

"A bit, but that's not why I'm doing this, Con. I'm concerned for you, man, and I don't want to see you get hurt."

"Well aren't you all sweetness and light." *Battle lost.*

Brian didn't seem disturbed by my tantrum. Of course, he never did, and it was one of the reasons our friendship endured. He was the only person I knew who seemed unfazed by my many moods.

"I'll tell you what, bud," Brian said, "if this ends up being purely innocent, I'll never interfere in your life again. Agreed? You bloody well know if you thought I might be screwing up, you'd do whatever it took to set me straight, so don't fuck with me on this."

I lapsed into a silent funk. I reminded myself yet again I was going to have to get a better handle on my emotions. Questions swirled through my mind. My guts churned as I thought of Meredith lying naked beneath the Adonis. No doubt, he had a much larger prick than I did. Or maybe it was the domination thing. What was she hiding from me?

Maybe I should have been more forceful. Maybe she wants it rough. But would I like it rough?

Brian resumed whistling while he followed the car into the darkness of the country highway. There were few cars on the road but enough to hide his pursuit. Several miles up the road, the inky night swallowed the silver car when it turned right. Brian sped up, passed the cars he followed, and took the corner at high speed. The Camaro fishtailed.

"Fuck!"

"Hang on." He straightened the car out, pressed the accelerator, and shot into the night. Now we were the only one following the silver car. The man drove as if he were on a racetrack, and Brian sped up to keep pace.

I was relieved when car lights appeared behind us on the otherwise deserted country road. I was even more relieved when we drove into the small town of Inverhuron where there was a bit more traffic. The dark-haired man drove toward the lake and turned down the road running behind the lakefront cottages. We followed. The car following us turned. Brian slowed to let it pass. A third car turned behind them, and I relaxed a little now that we weren't so visible.

The convoy drove to the end of the beach road and through large wrought-iron gates. The outline of a large house showed through the trees. Brian pulled over. Another car passed us and disappeared through the gates.

"Looks like she's going to someone's cottage." I still hoped there was a logical explanation for this. "It must be a party."

"That's one fuck of a big house for a cottage. Anyway, I'm up for a party." Brian put the car in gear and followed the other cars. He wound through the tree-lined lane and stopped in front of the Colonial-style building the size of a small hotel. A doorman stood at the entrance and opened the door for a couple. A valet got into the Jaguar stopped in front of us and drove off. The other valet at the door approached our car.

"Oh shit." The fist in my guts clenched tighter.

"Oh shit, nothing, Connor. Follow my lead. And try to look a little less like you ate a rotten pickle." Brian fished out his wallet and pulled out a twenty-dollar bill. The valet opened his car door.

"Good evening, sir."

Brian handed the valet his keys wrapped in the twenty. "Take good care of her for me." He winked at the valet.

That Bri has balls.

We strode toward the house. I wished I had Brian's confidence and swagger. Brian not only looked as if he belonged there, he looked as if he owned the place. I straightened my shoulders and followed Brian through the ornately carved entranceway.

Inside, Meredith's driver stood behind a large cherry desk talking to the handsome blond man from Meredith's kitchen. *Brett Sandvine.* They both watched us cross the threshold. A spasm crossed my bowels. I couldn't help staring at Brett, who returned the look, his face inscrutable. I looked away.

"May I help you?" the driver asked, moving closer to the desk.

"Yes," said Brian. "We're guests of Meredith's."

"Meredith Kincaid." My tone held a confidence I was far from feeling as I met Brett's gaze. A smile tugged at the corners of his lips as if he contemplated a private joke.

"May I see your invitation?"

"She said she'd leave our names at the door—Connor and Brian."

"I'm sorry, this is a private club."

"I'll take it from here, Greg." Brett came around the desk and walked to a carved wooden door leading from the vestibule. "Right this way, gentlemen."

I hesitated for a moment. Going through that door could irrevocably change my life. Brian tugged at my arm and hissed, "Come on."

We followed Brett through the door into a large room filled with people.

"Let's get you seated." He made a small gesture, and a statuesque woman dressed in a black corset and heels joined us.

"Yes, sir?"

"Give my friends here a quiet table with a good view of the show, and get them whatever they wish to drink on me." He turned back to us. "Make yourselves comfortable, and I'll join you in a while."

Before I could stop myself, I burst out, "I know who you are. Why are you doing this?"

"I am more than pleased to meet you, Connor. As for your question, there is very little I wouldn't do for Meredith and her friends."

"How do you know we're friends?" Brian asked.

He favored Brian with a humorous look, reminding me of how adults look at a precocious child.

"You're here at her invitation, aren't you?" He nodded at the server and walked away.

The server seated us, took our drink order, and left us to inspect our surroundings.

Couples in various stages of undress sat around two rows of tables ringing a raised platform in the middle of a large ballroom. Although we were near the back of the room, we had a perfect view of the dais. Soft light from chandeliers shimmered on the polished wood floor. Thick burgundy draperies covered floor-to-ceiling windows, absorbing the sounds of music and conversation.

"Holy shit," Brian whispered. "This bar is dripping money."

"I don't think this is any regular bar." Like the man said, it's a private club. I wonder where Merry is?" I couldn't shake the cloak of foreboding dropping over me. *Where is she?*

"Yeah, where is she anyway? I want to get a good look at the woman who's managed to vice grip your balls."

I prayed she wasn't one of the couples sitting at the banquettes locked in various stages of embrace.

The server returned and placed our drinks on the table. "Your hostess will be with you shortly. Will there be anything else?"

"Not for the moment. Thank you." She took her leave.

"Not for the moment, thank you. Since when did you get so prissy?"

"Would you lay off me?"

Brian laughed and lightly punched me in the arm. "Lighten up, Con. Let's have some fun. I certainly plan to." He took a sip of the single malt scotch he'd ordered and smacked his lips.

"Man, this is good stuff."

The lights grew even dimmer. Symphonic music played in the background, and a hush fell over the crowd as a small circular stage drifted up through a hidden opening in the middle of the raised platform. The stage rose into view, revealing the sculpted back and firm, round ass of a woman tied to a large mahogany *X*. I went rigid, my hands gripping the arms of the chair. The glow of a small spotlight highlighted every aspect of her flawless skin. She faced the cross with her back to us. Padded restraints securely fastened around her arms and legs so she stood spread-eagled. Adrenaline shot through me when I caught a glimpse of a ball gag in her open mouth. She was stark naked except for the simple gold collar she wore around her neck. Brian whistled softly.

"Would you look at that. She's perfect." He didn't seem to notice when I didn't answer him. "Cool collar."

Confusion, anger, and humiliation flooded through me. I'd know that body anywhere. *I don't fucking believe it.*

A naked woman and man, both of whom could have been Greek gods, stepped onto the stage.

Oh my God, it's that Ken guy from the restaurant, but who is she? Asha? It's quite the incestuous little party they have going on here.

Both were statuesque, and they made Meredith's five-foot-eight frame seem petite in comparison. The red-haired Ken stood behind Meredith, and the woman moved in front of her. Meredith rolled her head from side to side as if trying to catch a glimpse of someone when the Domme placed a hand on the back of her head, holding it in place. Ken loosened Meredith's hair and examined her as if she were his chattel before he let the weight of it slide down her back.

"If you want to please me, you won't move. You do want to please me, don't you? Don't get me wrong, I want to see you struggle, and I'll give you plenty of reasons to. Until then, restrain yourself. You do want to please me, don't you?" Ken's voice rang out strong and clear in the stillness of the room.

My gaze remained riveted on Meredith's back. The woman grasped each buttock with her hands and spread the cheeks of her ass wide, exposing Meredith for all to see. My own anus tightened in response as tension radiated through me. I clenched my fists, ignoring the pain building in my chest.

"Breathe, buddy," Brian said in my ear, slapping me on the back. "What's the matter with you?"

Only my chest moved as I let out the breath I'd been holding. My attention remained fixed on Meredith's back, and I barely noticed the stunning young woman who sat at our table.

"Hi. My name is Asha. Welcome."

So it isn't Asha up there. Then who the hell is she?

"Brian Patrick Farrell, here. My God. Where have you been all my life?"

"And who's your friend?"

I ignored the chatter commencing between Brian and Asha. I was too busy trying to identify my swirling thoughts.

The Domme, wearing nothing but a leather collar and heels, leaned in, capturing the attention of the patrons, and said in a stage whisper, "I like showing you off." She paused letting utter silence fuel their anticipation.

"I love to play with you. You know why? Because I know you want me to. Look at me. I can see it in your eyes. Begging me to squeeze harder and harder. Wanting me to pull those beautiful cheeks wide open. It excites you to know everyone can see your ass, stretched open, inviting. Let's not disappoint them."

Meredith flushed with excitement, moaned through the ball gag, nostrils flaring, as if embracing the nails of the Domme's fingers digging into her flesh. Ken inserted a lubricated butt plug into her gaping anus. Stretching her even further, it penetrated to a depth I didn't think possible. The Domme let go of her cheeks, and they closed on the probe, trapping it in place.

I instinctively rose from my seat when the woman picked up a riding crop and delivered several stinging slaps to Meredith's toned buttocks. A firm hand gripped my shoulder.

"She's here because she wants to be." Brett's voice was so low I strained to hear it before I slumped back into my chair.

"How can you be so sure?" I half turned, looking into his penetrating gaze.

"Meredith needs this as much as she needs air." He melted back into the crowd.

Ken grasped Meredith's wrists. The red hair on his

muscular chest brushed against her back, and his stiff cock slid through the wetness flowing down her thighs.

"Time for a little pole dancing." He plunged into her, his huge cock nearly splitting her in half.

My fists clenched even harder when Meredith's back arched with desire as the Adonis drove his enormous condom-covered phallus into her.

Fuck. Fuck. Fuck. Business meeting, my ass. Why did she lie to me? Why?

8

My first thought was to leave, but something kept me glued to the chair. My emotional discomfort conflicted with the realization I was as hard as a rock.

"Look at me." The Domme's steel tone reverberated in every corner of the large room. "I want to watch you come, but not until I'm ready. Let's see if you're the submissive they say you are or some little plaything who likes to play games."

She sought and found Meredith's engorged clit, squeezing it between her left thumb and index finger.

The shock elicited a high-pitched moan from Meredith. She writhed as if trying to control her body's need for release. The thick cock thrust in and out of her tight sheath with increasing speed. The Domme stared into Meredith's eyes, challenging her with each firm stroke on her clitoris. Meredith bit down on the gag, clearly trying to hold off the inevitable. Tears of effort rolled down her cheeks.

"Wait for me, sweet thing," said the Domme. Only then did I realize the Domme was groping herself.

"Are you ready to come? Do you need to come? Will you

scream for me?" The Domme panted the words as she neared her own climax. "Then scream. Now!"

The Domme's fingers raced across the shaft of Meredith's clitoris, pumping it with a frenzied rhythm. The cock sliding into her from behind pushed deeper, over and over. She screamed long and loud. Not even the ball gag could hold back the intensity of her eruption. I thought I heard Ken say, "Now I own you," but in my torpor, I might have imagined it. Not that it mattered. Meredith seemed beyond caring about anything but the rapture consuming her.

Meredith's scream of release still vibrated through me. My desire turned to anger as the crowd burst into applause and appreciative whistling, Brian right along with them.

"Wow! That was spectacular. What a beautiful woman. And public fucking. Wow." Brian continued clapping enthusiastically. "Now that's entertainment."

"You liked that, did you?" Asha asked. "Give me a minute, sugar. I'll be back."

I sat and glowered.

"What is wrong with you, man?"

"That was Meredith, you asshole. Don't you get it?"

"Really? Interesting. And now you know what she does for business."

"Fuck off, Brian! You really are an asshole."

"Now wait a minute, Con. Don't take your temper out on me."

"You're as bad as the rest of these idiots."

"If it had been anyone else, you would have said I could learn to love somebody like her. Now listen to you."

"You don't get it, do you, Brian?" My voice dripped tension. "This is different. She's mine."

"Listen to yourself, you hypocritical, self-absorbed piece of shit. What the hell makes you think you own her? News flash, Connor, you don't. You think she's up there doing this to humiliate you? Grow up. For a smart man, you're not too goddamn bright."

I stood, knocking back the carved wooden chair. It almost trips a server navigating her way through the bustling crowd as people took advantage of the intermission. She swerved and expertly balanced a loaded tray above her head. I set the chair upright and glared at my friend.

"Give me the keys."

"I don't think so, buddy. You're not driving my baby when you're in this mood. I'm waiting for Asha."

"Oh great. Another night of listening to you with another of your little sluts."

"Okay, that's enough. You'd better go cool off before we both say something we'll regret."

I glared at Brian. I couldn't remember a time when he'd stepped back from me. I was lost in my emotions. Pushing through patrons who were unfortunate enough to get in my way, I bolted for the door.

I stumbled across the stone patio at the back of the large estate. I gulped the cool night air, trying to get rid of the large lump threatening to choke off my breathing.

This is why I hate feelings. Hate them. Hate them. Hate them!

I gazed into the night sky. For a moment, nothing existed in my universe except the enormity of nature and my breaking heart. A solitary cloud drifted across the face of the full moon. The shimmering moonlight darkened, matching my mood.

Several minutes passed before I became aware of the smell of cigarette smoke drifting from the shadows beside me. The hair stood up on the back of my neck. I spun and saw the outline of a man slouched against a low wall. He wore jeans, an open shirt, and loafers. His arrogant smile obviously contrived to belittle others and remind them of his superiority.

"That's right, little man. It's me, Ken. I thought that was you." He came away from the wall and took his time grinding the cigarette butt with the toe of his shoe.

"So, how'd you like the show? She's magnificent, isn't she? But rumor has it you know how talented she is. I would imagine she played you for whatever she wanted. How does it feel to be her latest boy toy?"

Bile rose in my throat as I faced him.

"Huh. You really believed it was more than the little slut satisfying her insatiable need, didn't you?"

"Don't you dare talk about her like that, you complete fucking asshole." My fists clenched and unclenched at my sides.

Ken laughed. "I can talk about her any way I want, little man. I plan to own her. If you're lucky, I might let you fuck her once more, but I get to watch."

A film of dark red slid over my eyes. I lunged, but Ken was ready for it. His fist shot out, catching me just below my rib cage. I fell to my knees, folding neatly in half with arms clutching my guts, and tried to catch what was left of my breath. My humiliation worsened as Ken laughed at me.

Brian's sneakers rushed into view then planted, wide apart, in front of Ken.

"Why don't you pick on someone your own size, asshole?"

If I hadn't been doubled over in pain, I might have laughed. I pictured Brian confronting Ken, fists raised. One thing about Brian, he never shied away from a fight. He wasn't as big as Ken, but he was fast. As my breathing eased, I moved from the fight zone to support myself against the garden wall.

"Oh really, ant? You want some too?" Ken threw a punch at Brian's chin. Brian dodged and returned with an uppercut that met the sheet metal of Ken's abs. The man didn't even wince. He smiled and watched Brian dance. Brian stilled, braced on his toes, watching for Ken's counter attack. With the speed of a cat playing with a mouse, Ken slapped Brian's face and twisted a lock of his long black hair around his fist. He spun Brian around and placed a massive forearm around his throat.

"Come to papa, sweetheart," Ken crooned in Brian's ear. "Let papa show you what a real man is like."

The next few seconds were a blur of activity. Brett gripped Ken's wrist and bent his hand backward, lessening Ken's grasp on Brian's throat. Then, Brian stomped on Ken's instep and rolled out of his grasp. Ken spun around, ready to throw another punch, but Brett's raised hand stopped him in his tracks. Intense satisfaction washed over me as Ken's face morphed from red to purple.

"I'll take it from here, gentlemen. Thank you. Come along, Ken. We have some business to take care of."

"Oh my God, Brett. When did you get back?" Meredith strolled into view followed by the woman named Asha. The ankle-length teal silk dress Meredith wore accentuate each curve. I wasn't sure whether the rush of adrenaline came from desire or rage. I couldn't take my eyes off her.

"Connor? Ken? What's going on here?" Meredith looked at each of us before returning her attention to Brett.

"Nothing for you to worry about, Meredith. Ken and I were just leaving. And your friends here came looking for you. Come along, Ken." With apparent ease, Brett turned Ken and led him toward the side of the house. The hold he had on Ken's wrist looked deceptively light, like a parent holding a child, but the pain etched on Ken's face told another story.

Asha moved to Brian's side and gingerly touched the cut on his cheek.

"Oh my. You're bleeding. Here, let me." Asha raised herself to her toes and dabbed at the blood with a tissue before placing a gentle kiss on the darkening bruise. "Thank goodness it's just a scratch. That ring of his could have done real damage."

Meredith planted herself in front of Connor, arms akimbo.

"What in hell are you doing here, Connor, and how long have you been here?"

"I could ask you the same thing, except I know how long you've been here." Another haze dimmed my vision as the demon of rage took firm hold. "So, do you slut it out often?"

"What did you say to me? I don't think I could have possibly heard you correctly."

"Oh, you heard me, all right. And just so we're clear, I asked how long you've been whoring around with the beach crowd."

A wave of crimson rolled up Meredith's neck and face, highlighting the roots of her hair. She shook the mane of glossy curls and took a deep breath.

"Look, Connor, I can see you're upset—"

"Upset, is that what you call it? Oh, I think I'm a little more than upset. How do you think you'd feel if you walked into a bar and saw me on stage fucking everyone in sight?"

"I don't know, Connor, but I certainly wouldn't have your holier-than-thou attitude. No, I think I'd get excited and want to jump your bones. If you'd let me explain—"

"Explain? Okay, Meredith, you go ahead and try to explain this one away." My tone bit through her, releasing the venom behind my words.

"If you can stop overreacting, we can talk this out. Please, Connor. You're acting as if I lied to you or something."

"Really. I'd say hiding the fact you're the headliner at a slut rally and calling it a business meeting is far from what I'd call being truthful."

Meredith stared back at me; shock and hurt leaked from every pore on her body. *Touchdown!* Dared I hope there was some guilt mingled in there? She released a breath between her full lips. A small tear ran down her cheek, as if she realized the loss of something for which she'd grieve for a long time. She turned on her heels and walked back through the open French doors.

"That was a little harsh even for you, Connor," Brian said.

"Keys." I stretched my hand out. I struggled to appear casual, but the cords on my forearms along with the tightness of my voice showed otherwise.

"They're with the car. Ask the parking guy to bring the car around. I'll be there in a minute." Brian turned back to Asha. "Thanks for your help. Maybe we could get together again sometime."

Asha tucked a piece of paper in his shirt pocket. "Any time you wish, slugger."

I couldn't wait to get as far away from this place as possible. Jumping into the car, I took off. I was hurt, humiliated, and mad as hell.

9

I lay on a lawn chair, wearing a dark-blue Speedo, sunglasses, and suntan lotion, brooding about the night before when Meredith rounded the corner of the cottage. She was holding out a Tim Hortons coffee as if it were a peace offering. Something about her, body and soul, pulled me like a magnet, and I fought to push those feelings aside. I didn't move a hair, except to swivel my gaze toward her. Was the chill I radiated my imagination? She cleared her throat.

"Connor, can we talk?" She placed the coffee on the small table beside my chair.

Silence reigned for a beat, then two, then three. After what seemed a lifetime of her standing there waiting for me to answer, she perched on the edge of a nearby chair.

"Did you hear me?"

In one swift movement, I sat up, turned to face her, and pushed my sunglasses on my head. My eyes blazed with anger.

"I have nothing to say to you. I think your little performance last night speaks for itself."

"Connor, I—"

She couldn't say it; she just couldn't say it. Every muscle in her body reached for me. Her need for me seeped from every pore.

"Connor, I—what?" My nostrils flared, but I spoke in a carefully controlled, mocking tone. "Connor, I like being a slut for everyone to see? Connor, you were another notch on my belt?"

"That's not true, and you know it." Meredith's anger rose in response. "I care deeply for you."

"Yeah, right. You certainly have one hell of a way to show it. I have nothing more to say to you, Meredith." I swept a contemptuous gaze over her and lay back on the lounger. I dropped the sunglasses to my nose, placing a shield between us.

"Won't you hear me out?"

I said nothing.

"Please?"

Again, nothing. After a few more tense moments, Meredith rose and left. I watched her walk away, wondering whether she'd look back. She didn't.

I spent the next week wallowing in self-pity. I spent my days in bed and my evenings on the patio listening to ballads about losing love while drowning my despair in the bottom of many rum bottles. After a few days of this, fueled by alcohol, I managed to convince myself I wouldn't think about Meredith. However, that conviction was as deceptive as finding the answer in a bucket full of booze. There were those first few minutes when I woke, late in the afternoon, remembering, and another piece of my heart broke. If misery loves company, I was quickly becoming his best friend.

"You aren't fooling anyone, you know," Brian said. He kicked the leg of the lawn chair I lay on. My eyes flew open, challenging the intrusion.

"What the fuck are you talking about? Can't a guy take in a little sun in peace?"

"You're right, Con. I'm sure getting a suntan is the remedy for stupidity. Besides, I wouldn't call late evening prime sunbathing time. Why don't you get over yourself and talk to her?"

"Why is that any of your business?" The last thing I wanted was to be brought back to reality. I was heavily into feeling sorry for myself in my dark dungeon of depression. I took a long pull on my rum and Pepsi, the only sustenance I'd had in a couple of days.

"Have you eaten or are you trying to kill yourself by alcohol poisoning?"

"What are you now, my mother? Why don't you leave me alone? I was just fine without your interference."

"Just fine, my ass. You haven't shaved or bathed in more than a week, and quite frankly, Connor, your moping puss is getting old. And if you don't go back to work, you're going to get your ass fired. How long do you think you can go on like this?"

"For as long as I want." I winced at the whining tone of my voice.

"All I can say is you're both quite the pair. You, trying to drink, starve, or burn yourself to death and she, trying to drink herself to death."

I tried to remain still, but my fist tightened reflexively.

"Aha, you do care. Go ahead—ask."

"You would be wrong. I couldn't care less."

"Yeah, right. I saw you flinch, and you're sounding like a two-year-old who didn't get his way. You'd better figure out why she has gotten under your skin. Think about it. This is more than simple jealousy."

"So you'd be okay if it had been Asha onstage treating all and sundry to that little show." My muscles tensed as I bit out the words. *I am going to have to get control of these involuntary body movements.* I willed myself to relax back onto the lounger.

"It's not like I'm married to Asha or anything, so yeah, I do think I'd be okay with it. I hope I'd be able to admit to myself it excited me and I might be into doing something like that myself. If someone like Meredith wanted me, I'd hold on and enjoy the ride. That's exactly what I'm doing with Asha." A soft smile lit Brian's face. "I've never met a woman like her, and you know I've had a few more than I care to remember. She's smart as a whip and funny. I could watch her forever even if she decided she wanted to have sex in public. She makes me want her and only her."

"Good thing I'm not you, then. I'm not even remotely interested in having sex in public."

"Really, Con? Since when did you become so self-right-eous? You're okay with watching it in public. I repeat what I told you the other night—if it had been anyone else up there, you'd have been all over it. You've been the one pushing to go to the strip clubs, not me."

Another voice joined ours. "Actually, I'm surprised. It's unusual for a Scorpio to be such a prude. Maybe it's time you stop hiding from your own sexuality."

Our heads spun to the source of the voice, stunned to see Brett Sandvine leaning against the privacy fence as if he'd materialized out of nowhere.

"You're not my boss, and I don't recall asking for your opinion." *Brilliant, Connor.*

"Call me when you're ready to be your own boss."

I stood and faced him. "Is there something we can do for you—Brett, was it?"

A small twinge of satisfaction flit through me at the glacial quality of my tone, but his answering smile spoke volumes about the childish game I played.

"You're right. You are none of my business. However, Meredith is my business, and I'm trying to find her. We have something important to discuss." A frown creased Brett's brow and his fatherly concern pissed me right off.

I opened my mouth to protest when Asha came rushing around the side of the cottage.

"He's got her. He's got her!" She was out of breath and could barely speak. Brian took her arm and led her to a chair.

"Who's got who?"

"Ken. Ken's got Meredith. He put her in his car and drove off with her, and she's stinking drunk."

I threw Brian an I-told-you-so look. More of Meredith's true colors were showing. Brett swore under his breath.

"Slow down and tell us the whole story." He sat in the chair opposite Asha. She sat, stood, wrung her hands, sat, and took two deep breaths.

"Meredith and I were having a drink at Gilley's Bar. I decided I'd better go with her to make sure she was all right. I've been worried sick about her. Anyway, Ken came and sat at our table. He handed Meredith a shot and started telling her about how he's admired her from the first moment he laid eyes on her and a bunch of other crap like that. He told her he could show her an even better time if she'd give him a chance."

"Not interested," Meredith slurred. She threw back another tequila and bit into a piece of lemon before throwing it limply on the table. Ken watched her with a cocky tilt to his head.

"What are you smirking at?" Meredith asked.

"I'm not smirking, sweetness. I'm wondering how your boyfriend could say such rotten things about you."

Asha came to her rescue. "Bullshit. He never said anything of the sort."

Ken gave Asha a malicious look he took care to hide from Meredith. "You weren't there. Maybe you should get your facts straight."

Meredith took a gulp of her beer. "What are you talking about, Ken? Brett says . . . Brett says"—she pointed an unsteady finger at him—"you were the one who instigated the fight."

"Fight, my ass. It took one punch to shut that foul mouth. I know I shouldn't have done it, but I couldn't stand to hear him talk about you that way."

"You're lying, and you're not welcome here, so get lost," Asha said, but the seed of doubt was already planted in Meredith's mind. She was still hurt by how Connor treated her when she'd tried to talk to him about what happened.

"You know I'm not," Ken said. "He really didn't like seeing you perform for the crowd, and—"

"Brett told you to stay the hell away from us," Asha said.

"He said nothing of the sort. You've all blown this little incident out of proportion. Connor was rude, and I set him straight. Look, Brett and I talked when things calmed down, and once he understood the situation, he apologized."

Asha stood, fists clenched and half raised as if she were going to hit Ken. She grabbed Meredith's arm. "Come on, Mer. We're out of here."

"I'm not ready to go yet." She took another swig of beer. "I'm . . . going . . . to . . . finish . . . my . . . drink."

Asha knew there was little she could do to change Meredith's mind when she was in one of these moods.

"Okay, if you insist. I'm going to find a phone and ask Brett to send his driver. I'll be right back." As she walked away, Ken turned his attention back to Meredith.

"Come on, babe. Let's get out of here. Or are you some

kind of little kid who has to wait for her daddy to come rescue her?" Ken said.

"He's not my father," Meredith said. "I just don't think I want to go with you."

"Won't you give me a chance to make this up to you?

"I don't—"

"You won't be sorry. Now bottoms up."

Although the room was already spinning, Meredith picked up the beer and downed it. She was beyond caring what happened to her as long as she didn't have to think anymore.

Ken stood and reached out a hand. "Come on, baby."

Meredith grabbed his hand, and he pulled her up. She stood a second and then slumped against him.

"Connor," she murmured against Ken's neck.

"That's right, baby, it's Connor. Come along now."

She reached up and put her arms around him. Connor was back. Everything would be all right now.

She thought she heard Asha yelling as he dropped her in the front seat of his car, but she could barely keep her eyes open. The car sped away before she could be sure.

"When?" Brett asked.

"Over an hour ago. I couldn't get you on the phone, so I came here. Mer isn't thinking clearly. She knows Ken's trouble, and I don't think she went willingly. She's so drunk. She doesn't know what she's doing."

"Where's the phone? We've got to get her back before they leave the country. Where's the goddamn phone?" Although Brett's demeanor was sharp and efficient, an undercurrent of panic weaved through his words.

Adrenaline rushed through me. I pointed toward the cottage. "It's in the kitchen." *Leave the country? What the fuck?*

10

Brett disappeared through the screen door in a few long strides. We followed, dumbfounded, and listened while he made the call.

"Greg, he got her before I could warn her." Brett listened for a moment. "Asha says it was an hour or so ago." More listening. "Did you get an address?" Pause.

"Got it. Let's rendezvous on the highway." He hung up without ceremony.

"What's wrong?" Asha asked.

"Let's go." Brett headed toward the door. We followed him, and I marveled at the man's ability to herd us. He exuded a calm, quiet control I admired—no, revered. We piled into his Toyota Land Cruiser. I jumped in the front, and Brian and Asha climbed in the back. The doors weren't even shut when Brett threw it in gear and sped off.

"What the fuck's up?" Brian demanded, leaning forward in his seat. "Where are we going?"

"Ken's got Meredith," Brett said.

"Yeah, got that," said Brian.

Brett threw him a look in the rearview mirror. Brian

slouched back in his seat and pulled Asha into his arms. He winked at me. I was grateful he was here.

"As I was saying, Ken's got Meredith. I just found out he has connections to the sex trafficking trade. He's an international slimeball. He has several aliases and never stays in one place for long. He seems to specialize in procuring exceptional beauties like Meredith for wealthy clients. Her love of sex and her need to be dominated make her an attractive target. I'm afraid he's going to sell her to the highest bidder."

I went rigid. My stomach held the weight of Mount Vesuvius, and I could barely catch my breath. *This can't be true. This* can't *be happening.*

"How do you know this?" I fought for some semblance of calm.

"It's what I do. I make it a point to know everyone who may affect my world. Unfortunately, Ken did a good job of burying his past, and he flew in under my radar. It took some digging to track down his background."

Night dropped around us like the tightening circle of despair threatening to stop my heart.

A few miles up the highway, he pulled to the side of the road. I saw nothing but darkness. Then, briefly, a flame flickered in the night ahead.

"Wait here. I'll be right back." Brett's tone left no room for discussion. A glimmer of the full moon peeked through a couple of cracks in the cloud-covered sky. He stopped in front of a man, who started to talk, gesturing wildly. Brian leaned forward in his seat.

"Shit. Isn't he the guy from the front door at the club?"

"I think so," I said, subdued.

In a moment, Brett was back, his return as silent as his departure.

"Here's what we know so far. We think Ken's got

Meredith in a cottage up ahead. He probably has some kind of setup he uses to subjugate his victims, and we have to get her out of there before he hurts her. So, listen up."

His tone commanded we focus because we'd hear this once.

"We think there are only two of them, Ken and his sidekick from the club. He has two black belts. We're not too sure about her, but let's assume she also has a martial arts background."

"She reminds me more of a kickboxer," Brian said.

"Regardless, you'll need to stay far away from both of them. Leave them to Greg and me."

"I need you three to find Meredith while we take care of those two. Don't react to whatever you see, just get her out of there. We'll worry about the rest later. No matter what you see, you get her out."

"Got it," said Brian and Asha.

"And you, Connor?"

"Count on it," I replied.

With the lights out, Greg drove his vehicle down a track cut through large fields of grain, and we followed. Several hundred feet ahead, we ran into the first electrified fence. Greg, whose car led the charge, stopped. He got out and opened the gate. We drove through and inched our way forward in the dark. I prayed. Not that I was a big one for religious stuff, but like most, I found it comforting in a moment of fear. Seconds became forever. We stopped again.

Two gates. More delay. Frustration swept through me, cloaking my fear. My thoughts whirled with implications conjured by the mysteries I was fond of reading. If this was anything like the books, it was not good and much too real. Once again, Greg opened the gate and we drove through.

We crawled along a twisting and turning sandy track until we could see slivers of light through shuttered windows in a structure ahead. Greg and Brett cut their engines and coasted to a stop. We left our cars. Greg opened his trunk and took out a gun and a bullwhip. He gave the bullwhip to Brett. Brett smiled. Asha gasped. I stared in disbelief.

"Don't look so shocked," Greg said. "This old girl's trunk is like a lady's purse. There's one of everything in here." Greg frightening intensity belied his casual banter. I was watching a man who believed he could stop an oncoming train by standing in its path. I had no doubt he would do just that and more for Brett.

"What's that?" I hissed, pointing at the gun.

"Serious stuff," Brian said.

"Don't worry, bud," Greg said. "It's a tranquilizer gun. Nobody's going to get hurt tonight."

"Maybe not by you," Brian murmured.

"Don't even think about it, Brian. This guy's out of your league. Getting Meredith is your priority."

"Let's go," I said. Impatience fueled my courage, and I started up the trail toward the house. If you'd asked me, I couldn't have told you what came over me, but suddenly, all that mattered to me was rescuing Meredith. *My* Meredith.

When we got to the house, we waited behind a couple of trees while Brett and Greg did a recon of the cottage. A few long minutes later, they returned. Brett motioned for us to be quiet and listen. His tone was low and intense.

"I see only the two of them in there. No sense of where Meredith is. Look downstairs first. They'll probably have her tied up. Release her and get the hell out."

Brian, Asha, and I nodded and followed them from the woods. We hunkered down behind a bush while Greg hammered on the front door. Brett waited nearby, bullwhip at the ready in his hand.

We took off for the back door.

"Yeah?"

"Police," Greg said. "We've had a complaint." That's all I heard before we were out of earshot.

As we sped toward the rear of the cottage, the back door opened, and the statuesque Domme from the club performance stumbled out, struggling with what looked like a large rag doll folded at the waist.

"Come on, sweetheart. Wakey, wakey."

We crouched and waited for the woman to struggle farther along the path leading to a cabin cruiser moored at the dock.

"We get her. You get Meredith," Brian said. I nodded.

Brian and Asha darted forward. It took a second for the woman to register our presence. She gasped, dropped Meredith in the sand, and ran with Brian and Asha in hot pursuit. They caught her and tackled her to the ground, careful to stay out of range of her flying limbs as she sought some kind of defensive purchase.

I ran and gathered a limp Meredith in my arms. I covered her naked body with my own, trying to shield her. Red welts covered her back, distorting the natural canvas of her flawless skin. I moaned as I rocked her. I heard a punch and a thud, and still I rocked her. Moments later, the steel of Brian's voice and his insistent grip on my shoulder brought me out of my stupor.

"Come on. We've got to go, Connor."

I lifted Meredith into my arms and stumbled back up the path. Part way, we met Brett and a limping Greg. Brett stopped us and took a moment to survey the damage. He took one of Meredith's arms and checked her pulse. I tightened my grasp, and a tight smile flitted across his face.

"Come on. We've got to get her back to the house."

"She needs a doctor," I said.

"I'll have my doctor meet us." He turned to face Greg,

"Bring Dr. Benson to the house." Without another word, Greg got into his Rover and left.

"Wouldn't it be faster if we took her right to the hospital?" Brian asked.

"No. It wouldn't," Brett said.

Brett threw open the back door of his Cruiser. When I placed Meredith onto the back seat, she moaned. Climbing in beside her, I pulled her head into my lap. Asha squeezed in beside me, and Brian jumped into the front. Brett spread a blanket from the back over Meredith's semi-conscious form. She curled into a fetal position and moaned again. Did she say my name?

"Would you get a goddamn move on?" I smoothed the hair away from Meredith's face. When she moaned again, I was sure.

"Connor."

"I'm right here, babe. I've got you. I've got you!"

"What the fuck is taking him so long?" I paced like a caged animal and muttered under my breath while I waited for the doctor to talk to us. Anger—at myself and the circumstances—competed with my feelings for Meredith and were tearing me up inside. I wouldn't rest until I knew she was all right.

"Dr. Benson is very thorough. She's in good hands. If there was a major problem, he would have called for an ambulance," Brett said. "Why don't you join your friends in the kitchen?"

"No thanks. I'll stay right here until I can see Meredith."

"Suit yourself." Brett went back to reading the newspaper. I couldn't understand how he could stay calm when Meredith lay upstairs in pain. I wished I could have controlled my emotions, but melodramatic was how I felt at that moment. I continued pacing and gnawing at my lower lip.

"She'll be okay. Her vitals were good, and her pupils were responsive. She's been drugged, but she's resilient, and we'll get her through this."

"How can you just sit there? And what about Ken and his sidekick? Shouldn't you be doing something about them?"

"Greg's taking care of them. He'll turn them over to the police."

It was as if I'd received another of Brett's there-there pats on the head. I sighed deeply and perched on the edge of a chair, willing my impatience into stillness. A moment later, Dr. Benson strode into the room, medical bag in hand. I leaped up.

"How is she?"

Dr. Benson raised an eyebrow and looked at Brett. Brett nodded imperceptibly.

"She's fine. She's out cold but should be awake in several hours." The doctor dropped his medical bag on a nearby table and took the chair beside Brett's. I took the chair opposite, completing the triad.

"I suspect she's been given the sedative called Rohypnol. You probably know it as the date-rape drug. I'll be able to confirm it when I get the test results back from the lab, but all signs point to that," Dr. Benson said. "From the looks of things, she'd consumed a lot of alcohol before ingesting the drug, so she could be unconscious for up to twelve hours. I should warn you a common side effect of Rohypnol is profound anterograde amnesia.

"What the hell—" Brett raised a hand to silence me.

"How long will it last?" he asked.

"With any luck, the memory loss will last less than twenty-four hours, but it could be permanent."

"You mean she won't remember anything?" I asked.

"She may not remember the events that took place while she was under the influence of the drug. She has some bruising and abrasions from what appear to be a whip. Aside from that, she should be fine, at least physically." He looked at Brett. "She may need to see someone."

"I'll have Dr. Petersen flown in if need be."

"Very well." Dr. Benson rose and collected his bag. "Make sure she gets plenty of fluids when she wakes up. Call me if you need me. I'll see myself out."

Brett shook the doctor's hand. "Thanks for coming, Jim. Sorry we needed to wake you."

"That's what I'm here for." Dr. Benson turned to face me.

"Goodbye, Connor. Meredith's lucky to have someone who cares for her as deeply as you do." He left the room. I stood and focused on Brett.

"What's this about a Dr. Petersen?"

"Sandra Petersen is a friend of mine and the therapist who treated Grasshopper when she was having trouble coming to terms with her sexual appetites. Depending on what happened to her, our Meredith may need someone professional to talk with."

"Grasshopper?" My voice dripped with vitriol, and my body shook with the effort of controlling my anger. "What the fuck kind of pet name is Grasshopper for an ex-lover?"

Brett stood his ground, cool blue burning through the depths of the fiery gray-green challenging him.

"Connor, making me the brunt of your fury isn't going to help anyone. Direct it where it belongs, at the people who hurt Meredith. You'd better get your anger under control if you're going to be of any help to her at all. She'll need your strength, and anger, like all raw, unleashed emotions, makes you come from a position of weakness. And let's get one thing straight once and for all—I never have been, nor ever will be, Meredith's lover. I've been her teacher, mentor, protector, friend, and confidant. I taught her how to maneuver in the BDSM lifestyle at her insistence and to save her from the danger she was exposing herself to. I've never had sex with her."

"What?" I took a step back as if I'd been slapped, confusion filling the gaps left by the anger draining from me. "But, I thought . . ."

"Well, you thought wrong. Sometimes it suits Meredith to leave people with that impression although I'm not sure why she'd play that game with you. Or is it an assumption you made?" Brett shook his head as if saddened by some character flaw surfacing in me.

"I apologize." I struggled to say the words needing to be said. "I know you care for Meredith. I don't know what's come over me. Thank you for your help." *Thank you for letting me take care of her.*

"Enough of this. I'm going to check on Meredith. We've left her alone long enough."

"I'll go," I said.

"Wait, you'll need this." He walked to the desk and picked up a bottle of lotion. "Cover the whip marks with this to help ease the bruising." I took the bottle and, without another word, strode upstairs to Meredith's bedroom.

She lay dwarfed by the enormous bed; her dark curls fanned the pillow emphasizing the pallor underlying her tan. I drew back the light quilt and winced as I saw the welts covering her abdomen, back, and thighs. I brushed the lotion on the welts. Meredith didn't move. I lay beside her, drew the quilt over us, and gathered her limp body into my arms.

As the hours passed, I held Meredith close. I stroked her hair as I sifted through my jealousy, anger, loathing, and the raw fear threatening to consume me. My heart pounded, nearly exploding, at the thought of losing her, and it stopped me cold. Yet I knew that wasn't good enough. It wouldn't be fair to either of us. Ignoring the pain of this self-examination, I fought on, forcing myself to discover the truth I'd done such a good job of hiding.

At some point, I dozed off. A movie of random images slid through my dreams—Meredith on the beach, Meredith smiling at me, Meredith giving herself to me, Meredith loving me.

I love her. I love *her.* In my dream, that realization resonated in a place deep within me, enveloping me with peace.

I awoke, startled, to a three-beat refrain penetrating the edge of my consciousness. *I love her.*

Meredith moaned my name and stirred in my arms. Cloudy ice-blue eyes opened and gazed right through me to a place only she could see. Panic overtook disorientation, and she started to struggle, lashing out at some unseen threat.

"It's me, Connor. I'm right here, babe. I'm right here," I murmured in her ear as I pulled her even closer. "You're safe now."

I continued to soothe her until she stopped struggling and curled into the safety of my embrace.

"Where am I?" Her voice was raspy as if she'd screamed so much, she started to lose her voice.

"You're home."

Meredith moved and winced. "Oh my God. What happened? Everything hurts." She sat suddenly. "I'm going to be sick."

I leaped out of bed, gathered her, and rushed into the bathroom, barely making it to the bidet before Meredith started to gag and vomit. My left forearm cushioned her from the cold porcelain while I used my right hand to gather and hold her hair from her face. When she was done, she curled up on the floor.

"I feel so dirty. I hurt so much." She started to cry, and it tore me apart.

I wasn't sure whether she was talking about her body or soul, or both, but I didn't take the time to think about it. I wet a facecloth and cleaned her face. I turned on the shower until the many heads released streams like a warm summer rain. I stripped out of my clothes, picked her up, and carried her into the stall. Using my strength to hold her, I rubbed shampoo through her hair, gently easing the tangles with my fingers. My guts clenched as I thought of the struggles that led to her knot-filled hair. Then, with great care, I washed every crevice of her bruised and battered body. Her tears became gut-wrenching sobs I prayed would pull the pain from her heart. I barely realized some of the moisture on my face came from my own tears as I absorbed her pain.

I held her there until the water started to cool, letting the downpour wash away the horror of the night before. Choosing one of her favorite towels, I dried her gently, careful to avoid the many mirrors, and applied more of the lotion that had magically appeared on the vanity.

When I took the loose silk shift hanging on a nearby hook and held it for her, she raised her arms, and I dropped it over her head before placing a light kiss on her forehead.

"Better?"

Meredith managed a weak smile. "I think so. I'm just tired."

I steered her back to the bedroom. Delicious smells wafted from a covered tray sitting on the table in the alcove.

"You'd better eat something."

Though she looked dubious, she sat numbly and let me feed her warm scones with all the fixings. When I was satisfied she'd had enough to help her regain her strength, I lifted her back onto her bed. She instantly fell into a deep sleep.

I picked up the tray and found Brett leaning against the doorframe. His smile radiated recognition of the love and concern we shared for Meredith. I walked past him, and he followed. When we reached the kitchen, I placed the tray beside the kitchen sink and faced the older man.

"So now you know," he said.

"So, now I know." A tortured thought hit me. "But will she ever be able to forgive me?"

The hint of a another smile flashed across Brett's face. "I doubt whether that will be an issue. The question is will you be able to forgive yourself?"

I turned to fuss with our dishes, placing them in the nearby dishwasher. "Where are Brian and Asha?"

"They decided to go back to the cottage and give you your space. Brian said to give them a call should you need anything."

I placed more dishes in the dishwasher. "And are Ken and that woman in jail?"

Brett paused, his expression one of frustration. "No. By the time Greg returned to their cabin, they were gone."

"I thought you'd hit Ken with your tranquilizer gun, and the woman was out cold."

"It's a mistake I won't make again."

I threw my head back and ran my hands through my hair. "I can't worry about that right now. I've got to get back to Meredith."

"I'll leave her in your capable hands. If you need me, I'm just a phone call away." Brett slid a business card toward me. I put the card into the pocket of my jeans and left to return to Meredith.

For two days, I lay beside her, holding her and saving her from the nightmares. The only reason I left her side was to get her anything she needed. I must have drifted off again, because I woke with a start to find her gazing at me through lucid and thoughtful eyes.

"You are beautiful when you sleep."

I smiled.

"How long have I been out of it?" she asked.

"A couple of days. How do you feel?"

"I'm fine. It's the weirdest thing, though, I can't remember what happened."

A shadow crossed Meredith's beautiful features. "I remember you watched me scene at the club. I remember you hated me."

"I didn't hate you, Mer. I was a jealous fool and angry you lied to me. Something inside me broke when I saw them touching you, and I went ballistic. That doesn't excuse my behavior, but I hope it explains it."

My excuse is that I love you. I lay stunned by my own revelation. I loved this woman, and I wanted her to be mine.

Meredith eased herself onto one elbow. She moved the tips of her fingers through the sprinkling of light brown hairs framing my chest.

I laughed and pushed her hand away, dropping a light kiss on the top of her head. "None of that now. We've got to get you better."

⁂

We spent the next few days eating, sleeping, walking, and talking while nature's healing balm took its course. I steered us away from any conversation that might bring my Merry distress. I kept things light, using my wit and cynical outlook on life to make her laugh. With each day, she grew a little stronger, a little less damaged. By the end of a week, her deep belly laugh told me she was on the road to recovery.

We lay drifting off after a day filled with sun bathing and laughter, when suddenly Meredith sat up. I willed my body to stay relaxed and waited.

"I didn't think I'd ever see you again. I was so afraid I'd lost you forever."

"I love you." My voice broke, and my gaze met hers in recognition of this new reality. "I want you. I need you more than the air I breathe."

"And I love you, and I'm sorry I lied to you, but I can't change who I am, Connor. I can't—"

I placed a finger on her lips, shifted my weight, and pulled her into the crook of my arm.

"None of that matters. The only thing that matters is the love we have for each other. I'm sorry I hurt you, but there's little merit in regret. I want to know you for who you are. We'll work this out together."

"But—"

I covered the rest of her words with a light kiss. She pulled my head down to hers, her kisses needy, urgent. I returned the kisses, reveling as her fervor spiraled through me like an arrow homing in on its target.

"Connor." Desire swam behind the love shimmering in her eyes. "I don't think I've ever wanted you more than I do right now."

Meredith lifted the silk shift over her head and lay back on the edge of the bed, opening herself to me. I slipped from my jeans and briefs, never taking my eyes off her. The look she returned was equally intense. I took a full minute letting my gaze roam over her body. Where some may have seen flaws, I saw perfection. I stretched beside her and kissed her softly. I cupped her full breast, coaxing the nipple to a hard peak. When it was fully extended, demanding attention, I took it into my mouth and slid my teeth along the sensitive flesh. Meredith responded with a sharp intake of breath. She stared at me, imploring.

I looked into her eyes, her pupils dilated with lust. I held her wrists above her head with one of my hands. She closed her eyes and relaxed into my understanding of her need to submit.

Our passion was raw and savage. Meredith spread her legs wide. I slid the fingers of my free hand between her nether lips, and the slickness of her arousal shouted her desire in a way no words could. I stroked, pinched, slapped, and teased the hard pearl, marveling at the way it stood at attention.

"Is this what you want?" I blew the words into her ear. "Is it?"

The thrust of her pelvis into my hand gave me all the answer I needed. I loved the way she writhed in need, her moans becoming short gasps of pleasure. Joy sprang through me as she crossed into the zone where she knew nothing but the inferno building in her clit and unfurling through her core. I brought her to the edge, repeatedly, and she pleaded for release. I took such pleasure in teasing her, playing with her body's overwhelming demands.

"Tell me," I demanded. "Is this what you want?" Is this what you need?"

She rocked her head frantically from side to side, unable to do more than moan her response. I watched, fascinated, increasing the pressure as I toyed with her rosebud, *my* rosebud. I waited, anticipating the familiar stiffening of her limbs signaling the onset of her climax. I was rewarded when she took one last deep breath and held it in, momentarily suspended in time before release convulsed through her.

I thrust two fingers into her tight sheath, letting the evidence of her ejaculation squirt over my hand. I found her sweet spot and pressed it against the wall of her abdomen, strumming it like the strings of a double bass. It took a few strokes for Meredith to reach another climax, this time shaking as the spasms tore through her. I kept strumming, and she kept coming. I worked her until she glistened with a sheen of sweat, tremors tearing through her.

Only then did I remove my fingers and massage my hardness, mixing my precum with her dew. Throughout, my eyes never left her. My mind melded with hers, my thick, stiff cock pulsing with every spasm rippling through her.

As if she were in sync with my thoughts, Meredith slid sideways on the bed and tilted her head over the edge, exposing her neck to me. She opened her mouth. I thrust into her, burying myself to the hilt, deep in her throat. She reached back under my cock, her fingers caressing my balls. They drew up tight and firm while she explored. With a slow, methodical rhythm, I pumped into her mouth, relishing the feel of her teeth sliding across the underside of my cock, admiring the beauty of this woman who willingly gave herself to me. Intense pleasure rolled through me, leaving nothing but a pure sense of happiness as our minds and bodies became one. I selfishly held on to that intensity as if my life depended on it.

After what seemed like an eternity of control I hadn't even realized I possessed, I withdrew from her mouth. She whimpered and lay panting. I walked to the other side of the bed, a man on a mission. I took hold of her ass, slid her to the edge, and took her. She groaned, taking me deep within her.

Her uninhibited passion fused with the shock waves rolling through my cock. For the first time in my life, love allowed me to expose my need for her as she openly surrendered herself to me. I threw my head back and roared my release.

I stood still, rigid, unable to move, my ragged breath matching Meredith's. She lay, eyes closed, her luxurious locks strewn around her head, framing her beautiful face. I would never grow tired of looking at her, knowing her, growing old with her. No matter what age and time did to us, she'd always be the image of perfection lying before me. *God, I love her so much.*

I fell onto the bed beside her and pulled her close, and the contours of her body melded with mine, the halves of the whole they were meant to be. Our breathing subsided to a harmonious rhythm, slow and even. We lay as one for a long time. Meredith was so still I thought she'd fallen asleep, but she opened her eyes, her face transforming into a curious expression.

"I still can't remember what happened. I can't remember how I got these bruises," she said quietly, her voice pulling me from my drifting thoughts.

I held her closer, willing her to let my body banish her demons while I think of what to say. A part of me had hoped she wouldn't remember at all.

"You don't need to remember. You're safe now." Concerned I was being selfish and controlling, I asked, "How much do you remember?"

Meredith thought about this for a minute.

"I remember going to Gilley's bar. I'd been going there and getting stinking drunk for days after that night at the club, so, I can't be sure I'm remembering the right night. The next thing I remember is waking here with you next to me and hurting all over. Why can't I remember?"

"The doctor thinks he gave you a drug that causes amnesia. He said it's probably temporary, and you'll remember soon enough."

"He, who?"

"What do you mean? The doctor?"

"No. You said *he* gave me some kind of drug. He, who?"

"That bastard, Ken."

"Ken? From the club? That Ken?" Meredith's voice shook.

"The very one."

Meredith ran a finger over the whip marks crossing her smooth, flat abdomen. "I'm not sure I want to remember. Why would he do this to me?"

"Because he's one sick fuck, that's why." The veins in my forearms bulged. I fought to keep the anger that was still too close to the surface under control. My arm tightened around her.

"Ouch!"

"I'm so sorry, babe." I disengaged from her and took the jar of arnica ointment from the bedside table.

"What's that?"

"Some cream the doctor left to help heal your bruises." I took the lid off the jar and knelt beside her.

Using the tips of my fingers, I started spreading the ointment.

"I still can't wrap my head around why he would do this to me."

"Brett found out he's into human trafficking. There's quite a black market for beautiful women like you in the sex trade. He thinks Ken was going to sell you to the highest bidder."

Meredith shuddered. I finished spreading the ointment and lay back beside her, wrapping her into my arms.

"I never would have let that happen." I pulled her even tighter. "I would have moved heaven and earth to find you."

"How long was I gone?" Tears sprang to her eyes. "Did he . . . ?"

Once again, I knew the question she left unsaid.

"You were gone a couple of hours, and the doctor says you weren't raped. We got you back before he could do too much."

Meredith shuddered again.

"I didn't think I'd see you again after you stormed out of the club."

I struggled within to find the words that would capture my remorse. I relented and told her the truth.

"I was a fool, and I hope you'll forgive me for my macho outburst. Sometimes I have a little problem with my ego."

The melody of her laughter took me by surprise. Meredith had a deep-throated laugh that made me feel as if bubbles of joy were rising through my soul.

"If that was a little problem, I don't ever want to see a

full-out tantrum." She ran her fingers through the fine hair decorating my forearm, raking her nails through it.

"No, you don't. It's not pretty."

My hand encircled her soft, full breast, resting over the steady beat of her heart.

"Other than the lie, what upset you so much?"

I rolled onto my back, curling her into my side, her head resting on my chest. I stroked the hair away from her face and, bending slightly, pressed my lips to her forehead.

"Like I said, I was a jealous fool. I didn't want him or his partner doing anything to you. I didn't want you on display for anyone else but me." I hesitated, swallowing, and decided to take the leap. I took a deep breath, willing myself to verbalize the thoughts I'd tried so hard to ignore.

"And, most of all, I didn't want to admit watching you with them excited me."

"Being with others is one way of helping me discover myself and the true nature of being a submissive. Finding you has made me rethink things. I don't want to be with others unless you want me to be. What I want is for you to be my Master, my Dom. I'll give myself to you and only you if that's what will make you happy."

I laughed. "I don't know about being a Dom, but I'm willing to learn. I want you to be yourself, Mer, and if that means you want to have sex with others at that club, I'll try to come to grips with it. But I need to know I have your heart, that your love belongs to me. I don't think I could live with anything less."

"You have my heart and more. I love you, Connor. Scening has nothing to do with love. It has to do with sex and domination."

"Knowing the true nature of your sexuality, and mine, means everything to me. I think I get that now. And if that's something you need, it's something we can try together."

"So what's changed?"

"I learned love has many mirrors, and I found our reflection in each of them. Something Brett said made me take a hard look at myself. He told me how important it is for you. He reminded me of how selfish I was and encouraged me to consider the true meaning of love. He was right. I don't want to be one of those people who live in their dysfunction, who never break free of the fears, insecurities, inhibitions, and walls they think protect them."

"And I don't want to be one of those people who simply survive, Connor. I need to explore who I am. I need to explore who you are. I need to explore who we are together."

"With your help, I know I'll get better at controlling my moods and not fall back into old patterns."

Meredith's laugh reminded me of the tinkling of fine crystal. "With my help, you'll learn to control me."

"There's nothing I'd like better." I rolled her over and rained her face with light kisses.

I took my time tracing every contour of her body with my hands and lips. With each suck and nibble, I paid homage to her strength and courage.

"You are so beautiful. I love you. I need you, and I'm afraid of what will happen now that I've opened my heart to you."

"I know. I'm afraid, too. But I love you, and when we love, we expose ourselves to all of those emotional pitfalls we try so hard to avoid. Love is never easy, Connor."

I let out the breath I'd been holding.

She loves me even when I'm a supreme jerk. She loves me!

"Don't break my heart," she said.

"I could never break your heart. I wouldn't want to live without your heart. Your heart makes the other part of the beat that makes mine whole."

When my fingers found the wet dew between her legs,

Meredith opened like a flower. I stroked her, each moan exciting me, each twitch of her body receiving an answer from my thick hardness.

"You bring out the best in me." In my mind, I became the maestro playing the instrument of her desire, leading her to the final chord, a chord that would resonate through the still air. I played the perfect chord, evolving from the rising crescendo and ending in the ultimate climax. Meredith's arched body hung suspended before collapsing as her surrender shook through her.

I positioned myself between her legs. She opened them wide, inviting me in. With one swift and graceful movement, I slid into her wetness while aftershocks still rolled through her. I stilled as the intensity of being within her, body and soul, filled me. I began, slowly, deliberately, worshipping her. Each stroke was a testament of my love; each stroke stoked the fire of her need. Her hips moved with mine, coming together as one. I watched her, amazed at the abandon with which she gave herself to me, never more sure she was a part of me.

Our opus continued, building to an explosive climax mirroring the power of our love. I folded her in my arms, never wanting to let go. Wanting that perfect moment to last forever.

"If I was to ask you, would you marry me?" I lay back on the pillow, my forearm shielding my eyes, heart pounding.

Meredith propped herself on one elbow and smoothed my cheek with her long, delicate fingers.

"Why? Are you asking?"

"No. I'm wondering what you would say if I did ask."

The silence was deafening as I waited for her answer.

"We'll see," she whispered, and I wasn't sure I'd heard her. I moved my forearm, and looked at her, guarded to hide the ray of hope shining through.

"What did you say?"

Meredith smiled and bent to kiss me, her hair stroking my face.

"Let's wait and see. We wouldn't want to spoil the surprise, would we?"

My smile burst like sunshine through a cloud. Uncontrolled excitement erased any hesitation I may have had.

"I want you. I need you. I love you. I want to learn and explore every facet of you. The possibilities are endless."

Thank you for reading *Teach Me*! Find out what happens to Connor that makes him swear off love in *Tempt Me*...

Prologue
Connor
Twenty Years Ago

I loved Meredith Kincaid with every fiber of my being. She was the one I was meant to spend my life with.

Then the accident changed my life and everything I believed in.

I gave her some flimsy excuse—I can't remember what—for needing to borrow the Porsche 914-6 to shop for a ring.

"You just want to go for a joyride." She laughed. "Take all the time you need. I'm going to bike down to the public beach. I need some exercise if I'm going to keep up with you." She dangled the keys and pulled me in as I reached for them, wrapping herself around me and kissing me deeply.

Several long, breathless minutes later, she cupped my butt and guided me out the door. I paused and took another look at her as she stood framed by the bright afternoon sun.

My God, she's beautiful! Yes, this was the woman I was going to spend the rest of my life loving.

I was thrilled to find the perfect ring in the beach town of Bayfield and eager to get back to Meredith. I cranked up the volume on the sound system and sang at the top of my lungs to my favorite Eagles tunes. Meredith was *my* sweet darling, and she was going to get the best of *my* love. Unsure of how I was going to do it, I was equally sure I'd propose that very night. Meredith was my world.

I came back to reality with a jolt when I neared Kincardine and saw a cluster of cars and people ahead. I pulled to the side and walked over to one of the bystanders.

"What happened?"

"Someone got hit."

"Are they badly hurt?"

"She's not moving."

"I don't think she's breathing."

"Has anyone gone for help?" I asked.

"Yeah. Some guy said he'd go to the nearest house and call an ambulance."

I pushed through the crowd to see whether I could help. The crushed remains of a bicycle lay beside the mangled front end of a van. For a split second, my brain refused to process the sight of Meredith lying curled on her side on the pavement.

I strode forward, pushing someone out of my way, knelt beside her, and gathered her in my arms.

She's only fainted. That's it. She passed out. She'll come to in a minute.

But her utter stillness and the trickle of blood oozing from the corner of her mouth told a different story.

I cradled her and screamed and screamed and screamed without making a sound. I remained frozen with her until the emergency crew took her from me. There were no tears and never would be again. My pain hardened into rage.

"Who did this?"

The woman crouched beside me shrank back at the quiet intensity of my voice. She stood and pointed to a man sitting on the curb holding his head in his hands, rocking and mumbling. I stood and walked toward him. The smell of alcohol fumes overwhelmed me. The man's mumbles became a chant: "It's not my fault. I didn't mean to." I looked at him, and the beginnings of a white-hot fury threatened to consume me.

I bent and whispered, "Even prison is too good for you. I'll make sure you pay for this the rest of your miserable life."

Tormented by the pain of my loss, I shut down and walled off the world. For just over a week, the only action I took was what I needed to keep me alive. At night, I lay on the bunkhouse bed and stared at the ceiling. My chest constricted and my heart tore, again and again and again. I stared at the unpainted planks adorning the far wall and saw nothing but my own tortured thoughts. During the day, I moved to the picnic-table bench in the tiny kitchen.

I couldn't function; at times, I couldn't breathe. Inch by inch, my emotions crawled a little closer to the room in the corner of my mind where I would lock them up and throw away the key. If loving someone hurt this much, it would be better not to love at all.

Over time, I accepted the fact life would never be the same for me. Any emotion I may have known reminded me of how pathetic and weak I'd become. That was about to change. I vowed I'd never allow myself to feel this kind of pain again, to believe in a world that callously tears you apart, seemingly without reason or the slightest hint of compassion.

At the end of ten days, I emerged, unshaven, ragged, and a little beaten down. I was determined to attain the wealth and power I needed to assure me complete control over all aspects of my future. Brett Sandvine, media mogul and my beloved Meredith's mentor, was just the man to help me. He made me his protégé. Under his tutelage, I transferred from medical school and completed a master's in business administration.

I'm not sure whether Brett saw potential in me or whether he took me under his wing knowing how much I'd loved Meredith, but together we built the media empire that was Magnum International. I became the son he never had. He taught me everything I needed to know.

Magnum grew into a powerful consortium beyond expectations. In time, Brett turned over control of the company to me and assumed the position of chair of the board. We were unstoppable. Being busy and successful filled the void. I had my work and my Masquerade Clubs. I had companionship at the snap of my fingers. It was easy to convince myself I needed nothing I couldn't control. All was right in my world, except . . .

Chapter One
Katherine

I hadn't thought about Connor in years. There were times the feel of his hand smacking my ass consumed my dreams. I had pushed those dreams aside. Oh yeah, no time for that nonsense. Yup, everything was tickety-boo, that is until my boss, Vice President of Editorial, Kevin Jordan, introduced me to the new Senior Vice President of Operations as one of Magnum International's star performers. I went rigid with shock.

Standing right in front of me was the drop-dead gorgeous Connor McClane, impeccable in what had to be a custom-made suit with a gray shirt and black tie setting off his striking, angular features—*trés chic*. I yearned to reach out and stroke that suit.

Forget the suit, stroke him.

Seriously, my heart went into arrhythmia. Cardiac arrest was imminent, and I wasn't sure whether it was seeing him again after all these years or how gorgeous he looked.

His left eyebrow shot up, and a charming smile spread from a pair of exquisite lips right through the rich velvet of his gray-green eyes.

"Star performer, eh? I'll have to keep my eye on you."

He shook my hand. His gaze caressed my body briefly before he turned his attention to the others in the group.

I saw a flash of recognition and longing jolt through him, but perhaps I read into it. Speechless, I stood and stared after the man I'd loved, and left, in our youth. He hadn't changed. Yes, there were subtle differences, but the fine hair on his arms still started in the same place on his wrist. His hair still had the silky curls I wanted to run through my fingers, and the sound of his voice still made me feel as if I were taking a bath in warm toffee.

I couldn't tear my eyes from him. I was fascinated by the way he motivated and managed the executive group and painted his vision for future growth with fluid grace and ease. He wasn't outgoing even if he could be quite animated when in the spotlight, but he was absolutely stunning with a magnetic personality.

The women on the team each tried their hand at engaging his attention, and I worked hard to control the annoyance shooting through me when they fawned over him. He stood back and watched. Although never impolite, it was evident he rejected their advances. He still seemed to prefer his own company. I relaxed a little; I had no right to be tense.

Looks like he's still as hard to get to know as he ever was.

Red-hot lust shot through my core every time I glanced his way, and I found it hard to focus. My attraction to him was as strong as it had been twenty years ago—maybe stronger, and it scared me. I took care to match his professional courtesy during any interaction.

Note to self: watch it, Katherine.

Exhausted from the effort of trying to appear nonchalant all day, I opted out of dinner and dancing with the group—a political *faux pas*, no doubt, but necessary. I'm an introvert at heart, and I detested having someone dictate how I spend my social time. I needed a few minutes away from the social roller coaster of the executive team meetings, so I grabbed a drink at the hotel bar. I ordered a long island iced tea instead of my usual red wine—not the smartest thing to do, but I needed a release from the pent-up energy driving me, source unknown.

Okay, yes, that's a big fat whopper. Connor was the source, as much as I hated to admit it, and seeing him again had sent me for a major loop. I sat at a small table in a dark corner of the room where I could watch the dancers unobserved.

A bolt of electricity raced up my spine as if the ions rearranged themselves in the wake of a shooting star. I looked up and recognized Connor's cat-like grace as he strolled over to the bar.

As he ordered a drink, I struggled to keep the intensity from my gaze so I wouldn't attract his attention. Then a stunning blonde approached him, stood on tiptoe, and whispered in his ear. His smile was a mixture of humor and cynicism, but he bent to listen. The old irrational possessiveness came flooding back as if it were yesterday. *If he's going to be with anybody, it should be me.*

His reply made the blonde tip back her head and toss her hair. She said something else to him, and he shook his head. I almost heard Blondie's "humph" before she flounced off. He smiled to himself, scanning the room before settling on one of the barstools. I quickly looked down at my table and sank further into the darkness of the corner booth, watching him out of the corner of my eye.

I signaled the server and ordered another "tea," intentionally oblivious to the effect the blend of triple sec, light rum, gin, vodka and tequila was having on me. When I reached for my wallet to pay for the drink, the server said, "It's already taken care of."

"By whom?"

"By me." Connor gestured toward the chair opposite me. "May I?"

"I guess so. I mean, sure."

I took another mouthful of my drink. *Jeez, Katherine, could you be any more articulate?* I blushed at my inability to think of something witty or clever to say. Try as I might, witty repartee always occurred to me after-the-fact.

"It's been a long time." I wanted to kick myself.

Connor held my eyes for a long moment and smiled.

"You left me without a word," he said.

Intense. Always to the point. *My turn.*

"And you never came after me," I retorted. *Came after me? Where did that come from?*

"If you'd wanted to be there, you would have stayed."

"Maybe." *Stalemate.*

I couldn't stop staring. He was exquisite. Those mercurial eyes gazed steadily back. The half smile that made a flutter of sunshine spread throughout my loins came and went. He undressed me with those penetrating eyes. I took another gulp of my drink.

More staring. It would appear he was still comfortable with silence. I most definitely was not, at least not with him. After what seemed like a lifetime, one in which I had more to drink, I looked at my watch and gasped.

"Oh my God. I've got to go. I'm giving a presentation in the morning."

As we got up to leave, I stumbled. *Oh shit, I'm drunk.* And there sat Mister Calm-Cool-and-Collected acting as if he'd been drinking his beloved Pepsi.

Connor smiled, cupped my elbow, and walked with me to my room. As we rode up the elevator, I fought the desire to reach up and kiss those luscious lips, afraid of rejection. I fumbled with the key card. He reached over, took the card, and slid it through the lock.

I froze. Every nerve in my body tingled. He pushed open the door and gave me the key. Those intense eyes undressed me. But I broke eye contact and walked into the room. When the door closed behind me, I released the breath I'd been holding. When I turned to bolt the door, Connor leaned against it, watching me.

"Let me see you." He spoke in a voice quiet with command.

Ignoring the dampness between my legs, I made a pact with myself—I was *not* going to allow this to happen.

"Connor, I'm not . . . We're not . . . I mean . . . It's been years since . . ."

I took a deep, calming breath. *Twit.* Here I was acting like the young woman I'd been on our first date, right down to the wetness spreading between my legs.

"Let me see you," he repeated.

"Um, give me a minute." I fled to the bathroom. *Get it together, girlfriend.*

I splashed cold water over my burning face in a vain attempt to sober up. I looked at the wide, brown eyes staring back at me in the mirror until calm settled over me. What to do? Should I send him packing? Did I even want to? *Wow, wait a minute. Give your head a shake.* Of course, I should stand up to him.

"Let me see you." The words brushed through me, washing away logical thought.

I kicked off my sandals and took an eternity washing my face and brushing my teeth, my mind at war with the sexual hunger burning through me. Part of me hoped Connor would get sick of waiting and leave. Part of me raced with excitement at the certainty of his command of himself and the situation. I straightened up with new resolve. If Connor was still there, I'd ask him to leave.

He sat in the corner, hands steepled under his chin, and looked at me. Under his scrutiny, I instantly became a schoolgirl again, a child who had disobeyed. He shook his head slightly and, with effortless grace, stood facing me.

"Come here." His voice was quiet yet full of command.

As if hypnotized, I moved in front of him. The tips of his fingers traced my bare arms. Goose bumps immediately sprang to the surface, and sexual electricity jolted through me. I lowered my head. He reached under my chin and forced me to look up, challenging me to react. He edged down the zipper of my little black dress and let it fall to the floor. Suddenly, nothing else existed outside my need to give myself to him, to have him take me, *now*.

The heat emanated from him as his fingers outlined the curve of my breasts. I shivered. I loved his hands. His touch reminded me of the thing I craved. Thoughts that filled so many sleepless nights. Thoughts that I avoided admitting to myself—to surrender to his will.

He hooked his index fingers in the band of my bikini

briefs and drew them down my legs, waiting until I stepped out of them. I did, like an obedient child wanting to please him.

Now I was naked and more than a bit self-conscious. Needing to do something with my hands, I reached out to unbutton his shirt, but he pushed my arms down to my sides, encouraging a passive acceptance of his control. I complied, allowing him to focus his attention on my breasts while I tried not to think about how I looked standing there. He played with each, first with nimble fingers and then with his lips. I couldn't stop the moan of pleasure escaping as more moisture built between my legs.

"Lie down and spread your legs wide for me. Don't move. Don't speak."

I started to protest. He put a finger over my lips and led me to the bed. I should have objected but couldn't. I closed my eyes and waited. That was the moment I surrendered myself to him, and I liked it.

"Watch me," he said. Again, his voice insisted he be obeyed.

I watched him undress. He had a splendid body, all smooth lines and sinew. I swear Michelangelo used him as the model for David, right down to the brown curls framing the sculpted lines of his face. His engorged cock sprang to attention when it escaped from the prison of his pants.

Naked, he straddled me and pushed my arms up over my head. I closed my eyes.

"Look at me. I want you to watch me watching you," he said.

Holding both hands above my head with one hand, he reached down with the other and pulled my nether lips apart and thrust his cock in straight to the hilt and rode me. He took his time, gliding his heat out inch by inch to the tip before burying it deep within me again and again. With each stroke, my clit brushed against his pubis, fanning the flames of my passion.

Each time my eyes started to close, he reminded me to watch him. Each command, like each thrust, drove me nearer to a frenzy so powerful I wanted to scream. His cock glistened with my essence, exciting me more. Nothing else existed except his body moving in mine. For what seemed like an eternity, he fucked me. I lay spread and captive to his will.

When I struggled with the need to come, he tightened his grip and continued his languid ride. He seemed to take pleasure in teasing me to distraction. Finally, he increased the tempo of his thrusts, and together our bodies convulsed in explosive orgasms.

"Alley Kat." His whisper was so soft I might have imagined it. Without another word, he slid out of me, got dressed, and left.

Some things never change.

I lay alone, relaxing in the afterglow except for a few unexpected quivers running through me. That was the Connor I remembered. Not so much the way he dominated sexually, but the obvious control and emotional distance he maintained. He was a man women wouldn't or couldn't say no to. It wasn't that you ever felt forced or intimidated. It was more the realization that if you resisted, he would only smile and walk away, leaving you wondering about what could have been.

He never kissed me.

He sparked an overwhelming sexual need that exposed every dark fantasy I tried so hard to hide. If I was honest with myself, it was a need I knew too well. One I avoided my whole life. My feelings for Connor threatened to break down my defenses, and that scared me more than I cared to admit. Sex was not the problem. It was those same secret fantasies, late at night, touching myself, that both tortured and excited me beyond reason.

I stumbled to the bathroom. The disarray of loose black curls framing my face mirrored my chaotic thoughts.

I can't believe I did it again. Yet if there were a next time, I would do anything he asked of me. *What on earth is wrong with me?* I was usually so decisive, so in control of my world.

I'd sworn I'd never be anyone's plaything again. Yet Connor drew me to him, like the proverbial moth to a flame. Just the thought of him brought a warm flush of desire to my core. I shook my head and put the evening's events down to the stupidity of an alcohol-fueled moment of weakness.

After all, it's only sex, right?

Wrong. I hadn't experienced such intensity since the first and last time I'd been with Connor.

I'd met Connor at university. Even then, he was cold, dark, brooding, smart, and one of the best-looking guys I'd ever laid eyes on. We started hanging out together. I hid the burning desire growing in my belly, convincing myself I wanted nothing more than a casual relationship. As much as he tried to hide it, my friendship was breaking through the emotional barrier he maintained with the conviction of a religious zealot. When I asked him to talk about what he was looking for in a relationship, he always passed it off saying, "Love isn't on my agenda."

Maybe it wasn't, but there was deep-seated hurt in his eyes when he said it, and I'd loved him all the more because of it.

In the ensuing months, to my growing frustration, he never attempted to sleep with me. Sure, he'd played with me, and there'd been some heavy petting sessions, but he never went beyond that. It was as if he was afraid to, which defied reason because his reputation for sleeping with almost every girl on campus was legendary. Our bond and our friendship deepened.

After graduation, everyone was celebrating at the local pub. Connor worked the room to the delight of the women vying for his attention. They reminded me of a pack of wild dogs fighting over the best piece of fresh meat. Okay, maybe that was a little harsh, but subtlety was never one of my strongest attributes. I wanted to kill every one of them, but all I'd allow myself to do was sit and watch him in action. So, no one was more surprised than I was when Connor walked me home. Just being near Connor excited me, not that I'd ever tell him that.

I was delighted when he accepted my offer for a nightcap. Of course, I chattered incessantly, hoping I wasn't coming off like a love-struck twit. During one of my tirades, Connor held up his hand, stopping me midsentence.

"Take your clothes off," he said.

I can't explain it, but the next thing I knew, I was standing naked and trembling at the foot of the bed. I didn't resist when he placed me facedown, extended my arms, and bound them to the metal headboard with a couple of scarves he pulled from my dresser. Pulling my legs apart, he knelt between them.

I was exposed and vulnerable. If it had been anyone else, I would have resisted. But it was Connor, and by this time, I'd have done anything he asked. My excitement showed as the wetness oozed from me.

His cupped hand slid under me and captured the full mound of my sex. I pushed down, sliding through the wetness saturating the palm of his hand. My mind and body raged with need when he closed his hand in a vicelike grip, capturing my throbbing clit between the engorged lips of my cunt. In one quick motion, he removed his hand, grabbed my hips, lifted me to my knees, and buried his cock deep within me.

With each stroke, he slapped the cheeks of my buttocks, hard. His hand molded the round globes of my ass perfectly. My flesh shuddered under the impact, and I was sure he'd left his brand with a red-tinged imprint of his hand. I gasped as each slap enhanced the pleasure of his hard cock. I lost control, completely overwhelmed by the unrelenting waves of pleasure pulling me to a climax of uninhibited abandon.

I came, for the first time in my life. Connor clutched the stinging cheeks of my buttocks, arched back, and pulled out of me, painting the cheeks of my ass with the outcome of his climax. He leaned over me for a brief second, and I'm sure he whispered, "My Alley Kat."

Without another word, he untied my arms, dressed, and left.

And there I was, a young, inexperienced woman wrapped in a torrent of unresolved anguish threatening to tear me apart. *Only a slut would let a man tie her down and take her from behind.*

Every bit of my moralistic upbringing rose to the surface, and the emotions overwhelmed me. I couldn't admit how much I'd liked it. My desire for Connor battled with my guilt and shame. Without experience or the perception that comes with age, my shame won out.

Damn my Victorian upbringing. How can I ever look him in the face again?

Left with no choice, I packed up my car and headed to anywhere else, and ended up where? Full circle, right back where I'd started with him. Except I was stronger now. This time, I had a choice. At least that's what I told myself, knowing if he had told me to beg, I'd have done so, and willingly.

He called me Alley Kat. He remembered.

The next morning, to my great relief, he acted as if nothing had ever happened. If not for the soreness between my legs, I could almost convince myself it hadn't. In truth, I wanted him even more than I cared to admit to myself, and I had no idea what to do about it.

End of Sample
To continue reading, be sure to pick up _Tempt Me_ at your favorite retailer.

ALSO BY LILITH DARVILLE

FOR A FULL LIST PLEASE GO TO LILITHDARVILLE.COM/BOOKS

Wicked Angels Series

Dark Urban Fantasy Romance

Interconnected Standalones

Follow a team of fallen angels as they fight against human trafficking and navigate the blurred lines between good and evil. Set in Pandemonium, a notorious club where they blend in with humans, this heart-pounding series will leave you breathless. Don't miss out on this intense and spicy journey of redemption and second chances.

.

Rogue Angels Series

Dark Urban Fantasy Romance

Completed Series

Rogue Angels is a twist retelling of the Snow White fairytale. Enjoy an adventure with fated mates, midlife crisis, and evil demons. This story includes themes of love, sacrifice, and self-discovery.

.

Sexy Sins Afterlife Retreat Series

Paranormal Reverse Harem Romance

Completed Series

Warning: This series has one strong woman and four dangerously sexy immortal men. She's been their fated mate in every life they've lived and they refuse to live one without her. Read this series if you like why choose romance with a paranormal twist and hunky guys times four!

.

Masquerade Club Series

Dark Contemporary Romance

Completed Series

A contemporary saga with a side dish of spice and a second chance romance for two people you'll never forget. The Masquerade Club is exclusive and available only for the ultra-rich where all your dreams and fantasies come true. Join the party and fall in love with Connor and Katherine in this angst-ridden suspense-filled series.

.

ABOUT THE AUTHOR

Lilith Darville is a *USA Today* bestselling author of dangerously delicious romance, including sizzling paranormal reverse harem. With over forty years of storytelling experience, her stories are guaranteed to make readers flush and blush.

lilithdarville.com

www.ingramcontent.com/pod-product-compliance
Lightning Source LLC
Chambersburg PA
CBHW020658120726
47906CB00001B/328